W9-BVG-542

Mr. Blandings Builds His Dream House

Center Point
Large Print

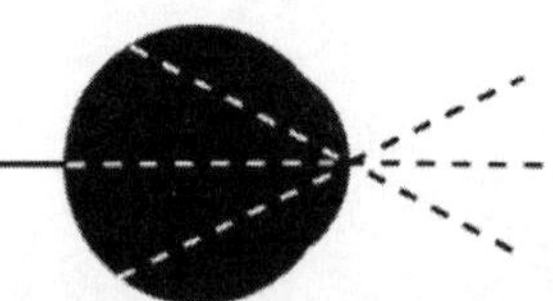

This Large Print Book carries the
Seal of Approval of N.A.V.H.

Mr. Blandings Builds His Dream House

ERIC HODGINS

Illustrated by William Steig

CENTER POINT PUBLISHING
THORNDIKE, MAINE

This Center Point Large Print edition
is published in the year 2011 by arrangement with
Simon & Schuster, a division of Simon & Schuster, Inc.

The text of this Large Print edition is unabridged.
In other aspects, this book may vary
from the original edition.
Printed in the United States of America
on permanent paper.
Set in 16-point Times New Roman type.

ISBN: 978-1-61173-120-0

Library of Congress Cataloging-in-Publication Data

Hodgins, Eric, 1899–1971.
Mr. Blandings builds his dream house / Eric Hodgins ; illustrated by William Steig.
p. cm.
ISBN 978-1-61173-120-0 (library binding : alk. paper)
1. Homeowners—Fiction. 2. House construction—Fiction. 3. Large type books.
I. Title.
PS3515.O1714M5 2011
813′.54—dc22

2011007830

To
RALPH DELAHAYE PAINE, JR.
Editor, builder, mortgagor

Acknowledgments

To my close and longtime friend, Albert L. Furth, Executive Editor of Fortune, *I owe a most personal debt for editorial services rendered Mr. Blandings far beyond the call of duty. I must have asked him to read the manuscript a dozen times in various forms and stages, and his suggestions for improvement were, alas, just as fertile and difficult to live up to in his last reading as in his first.*

The Messrs. Howard Myers and George Nelson of The Architectural Forum *were also kind enough to criticize the manuscript and several times helped me out of architectural holes I had dug for Mr. Blandings from which, it turned out, I could not rescue him unaided. To my friend Wilton D. Cole, Attorney at Law, I owe many helpful suggestions in the vast, dark domain of jurisprudence as Mr. Blandings encountered it. As for the Misses Renata von Stoephasius and Alice Weigel, of* Fortune *and* Time *respectively, each scrutinized Mr. Blandings with such a candid yet friendly eye that I do not know what either he or I would have done without them.*

E. H.

East Dennis, Massachusetts
September, 1946

Contents

BOOK ONE

BOOK TWO

Book One

I

The Real-Estate Man

The sweet old farmhouse burrowed into the upward slope of the land so deeply that you could enter either its bottom or middle floor at ground level. Its window trim was delicate and the lights in its sash were a bubbly amethyst. Its rooftree seemed to sway a little against the sky, and the massive chimney that rose out of it tilted a fraction to the south. Where the white paint was flecking off on the siding, there showed beneath it the faint blush of what must once have been a rich, dense red.

In front of it, rising and spreading along the whole length of the house, was the largest lilac tree that Mr. and Mrs. Blandings had ever seen. Its gnarled, rusty trunks rose intertwined to branch and taper into splays of this year's light young wood; they, in turn, burst into clouds of blossoms that made the whole vast thing a haze of blues and purples, billowed and wafting. When the house was new, the lilac must have been a shrub in the dooryard—and house and shrub had gone on together, side by side since then. That was a hundred and seventy years ago, last April.

"If the lilac can live and be so old, so can the house," Mrs. Blandings said to herself. "It needs someone to love it, that's all." She flashed a glance at her husband, who flashed one back at her.

Using a penknife as a key, the real-estate man unlocked a lower door. As it swung back, the top hinge gave way and splashed in a brown powder on the floor. The door lurched against Mr. Blandings, and gave him a sharp crack on the forehead, but the damage was repaired in an instant, and Mr. Blandings, a handkerchief at his temple and his wife by his side, stood looking out through the amethyst window lights at an arc of beauty that made them both cry out. The land rushed downward to the river a mile away; then it rose again, layer after layer, plane after plane of hills and higher hills lighter beyond them. The air was luminous, and there were twenty shades of browns and greens in the plowed and wooded and folded earth.

"On a clear day you can see the Catskills," said the real-estate man.

Mr. and Mrs. Blandings were not such fools as to exclaim at this revelation. Mrs. Blandings flicked a glove in which a cobweb and free-running spider had become entangled; Mr. Blandings, his lips pursed and his eyes half closed, was a picture of controlled reserve; strong, realistic, poised. By the way the two of them said "Uh-huh?" with a rising inflection in perfect unison, the real-estate man knew that his sale was

"You'd have to do a little pointing up here," said the real-estate man.

made. The offer would not come today, of course; it might, indeed, not come for a fortnight. But it would come; it would come with all the certainty of the equinox. He computed five per cent of $10,275 in his head and turned to the chimney footing.

"You'd have to do a little pointing up here," he said, indicating a compact but disorderly pile of stone in which a blackened hollow suggested a fireplace that had been in good working order at the time of the Treaty of Ghent. Mrs. Blandings, looking at the rubble, saw instead the kitchen of the Wayside Inn: a distaff plump with flax lying idly on the polished hearth; a tempered scale of copper pans and skillets pegged to hang heads downward near the oven wall; a bootjack in the corner and a shoat glistening on the spit.

What Mr. Blandings saw broke through into speech. "With a flagstone floor in here it'd be a nice place for a beer party on a Saturday night. You could put the keg right over in that corner."

He laughed a mild laugh which meant to say that if his thought was frivolous so, indeed, was the whole occasion that had called it forth. The notion that he might buy this old farmhouse, or any other, anywhere, ever, was light, gossamer nonsense; a whimsy; a caprice; it was his pleasure to give it a momentary fiction of solidity.

The real-estate man refused to take Mr. Blandings' suggestion so lightly. "You could at that," he said, awe and rumination mixed in his voice, as though he had just heard a brilliant restatement of nuclear theory. He quickly did five per cent of $11,550 in his head; aloud he said: "You haven't seen what's on the other side, either."

Mr. and Mrs. Blandings stepped across a mound of rubbish on the cold earthen floor and saw an even more impressive example of masonry in disarray. The second fireplace, loosely connected to the same flue as the first, stood at an angle with it that made a rough, bold V. Its stones were even more massive; hearth and manteltree were both huge monoliths. No frame of reference in all Euclid could be taken to which any major piece would be plumb, level, or square, but it was the work of a moment for Mr. Blandings to set everything to rights and swing a polished black kettle on its crane over the glowing ashes of an oak that he himself had sawn and quartered. In a moment he would have a mug of hot rum to banish the cold from his ten-mile plunge through the snowdrifts to rescue the heifer his hired man had abandoned for lost. . . .

"They must have done their slaughtering down here years ago," said the real-estate man. "You don't see an old kettle like that every day in the week, not even in this part of the country."

The Blandings followed his forefinger and saw, on a circular pedestal of stone to the right of the hearth, a huge hemisphere of somber metal. Mr. Blandings thumped it lightly with his fist and it gave forth a hushed, whispering boom. "I think they filled that full of boiling water and scalded the hide off the pig before they dismembered him. Anyway, they must have hung their hams and bacon flitches on those hooks up there."

Mrs. Blandings, the *membra disjecta* of whose broiling chickens came to her kitchen packed into neat rectangles from the frozen-food store near her city apartment, contemplated the slaughtering of a 300-pound hog with ease, and observed the slender beauty of the hooks sunk deep in the old beams; hooks that had been shaped and pointed on some anvil lost in the tall grasses of a century ago.

"Mind your head as we make the turn," said the real-estate man, leading his prospects into a gloom in which a stairway could be faintly discerned. "I want you to see the living room just the way it's been left ever since old Mr. Hackett died." Despite the injunction, Mr. Blandings failed to stoop sufficiently; a beam dealt his head a vibrant blow on the same side that had suffered a few minutes ago from the door. But his dizziness left him in a moment and he was able to join his wife in the admiration she thought she was concealing by her silence.

The living room of the old Hackett house was not quite anything the Blandings had ever seen before. Another huge fireplace jutted from the massive central chimney; it would have dominated the room, Mrs. Blandings was certain, if it had not been so carefully boarded up, and the boards plastered over with the same wallpaper that ran around the room from ceiling to floor, covering all moldings and ornaments of the past. The wide oak planks of the floor, rounded and buckled here and there, and the magnificent hand-hewn beams, were obviously unchanged since Revolutionary times. But the furnishings were in general of the era of Benjamin Harrison, with an overlay of William McKinley, and here and there a final, crowning touch of Calvin Coolidge. There had been here no self-conscious restoration, no museum hand. The old house had been lived in through successive eras of changing custom and invention and usage and decoration; here was the residue, left when at last one final patriarch had died, and somehow that had been the end of a long story.

A square Checkering piano stood in one corner of the room as the Blandings surveyed it; a slimpsy and betasseled throw still carelessly draped across its shoulders. Its keys were not ivory, but mother-of-pearl, and a book bound in faded green boards stood on the music rack: *100 Songs All the World Loves.* Two deeply tufted horsehair chairs were close by. One rested foursquare on its own feet; the other was a rocker that rocked not on the floor but on its own two tracks to which the rockers were held by an elaborate mechanism of tension springs, guide flanges, and curved restrainers, with which something was now badly askew. That was somebody's functionalism, once, thought Mr. Blandings, but without the depression that might normally have followed such an idea.

The Hacketts had been a music-loving family,

apparently. A phonograph of the up-ended-casket type stood by a window, a record still on its turntable. To Mr. Blandings' amazement it revolved when he gave it a push, and when he lowered the rusty tone arm, complete with needle, onto the record groove, the room rustled for a minute with the sound as of a deaf-mute singing *Dardanella* through a funnel. Then something metallic ruptured inside the simulated mahogany, and all was still again.

Mrs. Blandings was too busy to reprove her husband, as she usually did, for meddling with what should better be left alone. She was moving in and out of a confusion of other furniture to gaze at an assortment of photographs on the walls: a large bright-tinted portrait, in an oval frame, of an elderly curmudgeon slicked up to the nines; thin, glistening white hair, a mustache with the curvature of a hay rake, a bulging green tie that sprang from the notch of a collar four inches high. Old Man Hackett, the last patriarch, Mrs. Blandings surmised. He was surrounded in other frames by what were apparently other members of his family, some cowed, some truculent. There was a family group in and surrounding a surrey that must have been the height of country style in the 1890's, and in the background could be seen, neat and perfect in a morning sun, the barns that now, on the other side of the road, presented only an aspect of ghostly ruin.

"They just moved out and left things this way when the old man died," said the real-estate man. "I never knew him, but he must have run a mighty smart farm. After they buried him, his wife and son moved back down into the valley, and the place has stayed this way ever since. You can see for yourself, that was around 1926."

He handed Mr. Blandings an old newspaper from the top of a vast pile of aging printed matter in one corner. It was yellow and heavy creased, and its date was June 2, 1926. Mr. Blandings studied it for a minute in the hope of finding something of deep significance, but it told him only that the Sesquicentennial Exposition had just opened in Philadelphia. When he turned it over, it snapped like a wafer in his hand.

"What sort of price is the owner asking for the property?" Mr. Blandings inquired. The sham of his casualness was apparent even to his wife, whose preoccupation with a papery wasp's nest behind a picture frame was itself no masterpiece.

The real-estate man's response was casual, too, but it had the benefit of twenty years of practice. "I think he's asking $15,000," he said, "but if you want my opinion, I think you could get it for less."

He turned a gaze of steady, manly frankness on Mrs. Blandings. "Maybe for a whole lot less," he said, very quietly, and with a smile that Mrs.

"Maybe you could get it for a whole lot less," said the real-estate man.

Blandings knew he was not in the habit of using on everyone, "if he really took a shine to his prospective buyers."

Mrs. Blandings combined La Gioconda and Madame Récamier in her return gaze, and the real-estate man went on. "These country people, you know, they don't want to sell the places they and their families have lived in for a couple of hundred years to every Tom, Dick, and Harry that

"Let's go up the hill and take a look at your orchard," said the real-estate man.

might come up from the city and flash a big bankroll on them. They have a lot of feeling about their places, and when they have to let them go, they want to see people get them that'll, you know, sort of want to carry on with them in the same spirit."

The smile the Blandings exchanged with the real-estate man was partly in gentle condescension of country people, partly in dissociation of themselves from all other city people who had ever before come up from New York to Lansdale

County hunting for a quick bargain in real estate. It was a smile of perfect understanding.

The real-estate man let a little minute of silence go by, to mark the intimacy into which they had all so happily fallen. When he spoke again, it was as if he had put a precious instant away in his book of memories and was returning now, because he must, to mundane things.

"Let's go up the hill and take a look at your orchard," he said, clearing his throat. "There's a very interesting story connected with . . ."

The effect of the plural possessive pronoun was as a fiery liquor in Mr. and Mrs. Blandings' veins.

II

Meeting of the Minds

Mr. and Mrs. Blandings traveled back to New York in a heavy flush; in a flush, still, they sat in the New York apartment which had been home to them until that afternoon. It was home no longer; the old Hackett place on Bald Mountain was home, now. They wanted it as once, fifteen years ago, they had wanted each other, and the symptoms were much the same: ravishing desire at one instant; at the next, a sick slump into hopelessness that the desire would ever be fulfilled.

The Blandings had always been city folk. When Mr. Blandings, fresh out of Yale, landed his first job with an advertising agency whose offices, like every one of its rivals', lay within the shade of Grand Central, he had taken a little one-room-and-bath apartment for himself in the East Thirties. When, after a few years of menial writing he was promoted to be one of three special assistants to the harassed unfortunate whose title was Copy Chief, he had permitted himself to expand to two rooms, and moved to the East Forties. He had married not long after that; as newlyweds, Mr. and Mrs. Blandings took up quarters in the East Fifties. When their first baby arrived, they skipped fifteen blocks in one bold leap and moved to the East Seventies. There they stayed. Neither the arrival of their second child, two years later, nor a series of modest but gratifying promotions by the now celebrated agency of Banton & Dascomb had budged them a foot farther north. The Blandings children, happy in the creative, anarchistic, and sexual freedoms of a progressive school near the East River and adjoining an asphalt works, had felt small need for natural chlorophyll or ultraviolet radiations from the actual sun.

Suddenly, this whole mode of living had become unsatisfactory; Mr. Blandings was beginning to have what seemed like a very nice income. His name had not become a great name in advertising, but it had earned a considerable respect in the inner circle of the hard-working, highly competent, and deeply miserable men who wrote advertising copy and, in another century, might have written sonnets. While still a relatively young man in his profession, Mr. Blandings had been lucky enough to hit upon a three-word slogan for a laxative account that had broken four successive agency vice-presidents. So compulsive did these three simple monosyllables become, iterated and reiterated to the metabolizing public from magazine pages, billboards, radio loudspeakers (despite veiled warnings from the Federal Communications Commission), and skywriting airplanes, that within three years' time a fading cathartic had come to stand with Ivory Soap, Wrigley's Chewing Gum, and Campbell's Soup as one of the dozen most widely recognized and demanded brand names in America.

The happy agency had rewarded Mr. Blandings with several handsome bonuses, and had done most generously by him on every one of the semiannual salary reviews since the three portentous words had first occurred to him. The client himself made it clear to Mr. Blandings that if ever he wanted to leave Banton & Dascomb for greener fields, the account would go with him: indeed, if he were ever to set up shop for himself he could always rely on the Knapp account to be the nucleus around which he could build a business of his own. Mr. Blandings loathed his calling with a deep, passionate intensity, but he was not the man to forgo all of the advantages that seemed to flow so easily to a man who "had an account in his pocket." If a business of his own did not tempt him, something that he and his friends called "the good life" did.

About the time that a piece of Blandings' laxative copy won a Harvard Advertising Award for the exceptional power and beauty of its language, Mr. and Mrs. Blandings realized that not only could they now afford to expand their modest horizons, but that, in the eyes of their professional colleagues, they could not afford not to. They had begun a search for land and an old house in the country in a manner that was not only halfhearted but shamefaced; they were doing something because it seemed to be expected of them, not because they felt any true inner urge. Then, suddenly, the land fever had seized them; they knew, in a flash, what had been wrong with them all those years: the peace and security that only the fair land itself could provide they had left out of their lives altogether. From not caring who, among their friends and colleagues, might own what country sanctuary or where it might be, the Blandings became feverishly envious of the County Fair blue-ribbon winners, the Black Angus cattle breeders, the gentlemen dairy farmers, who had been finding rural escape from the advertising-agency business and the Grand Central Zone, even if only for week ends. And it had been just as they had reached a pitch of desperate resolve that somehow they must make up for one whole lost decade in their lives that they had come upon the Old Hackett Property at the top of Bald Mountain.

"Farm dwelling, oak grove, apple orchard, trout stream, hayfields, four barns, seclusion, superb view, original beams, paved highway, acreage, will sacrifice," *The New York Times* advertisement had said. As the Blandings saw it, it was all utterly true—all, that is, except the very last, which remained an open and terrible question. When the

Blandings tried to sleep that first night after their return from Bald Mountain, they could only thrash miserably on their pillows, tortured by visions of Ephemus W. Hackett surrounded by scores of jostling buyers, screaming to be heard. Actually, if Mr. Blandings could have known, Mr. Hackett was having a very quiet time of it: when last a city dweller had offered to buy what had once been his father's and his family's home, it was August, 1929. Some financial trouble in the cities had then ensued, and the deal had not matured; his friends had told Eph Hackett that he would probably have to wait a long, long time now to sell his property at the price he wanted. But here it was, less than a decade later, and the real-estate man from near-by Lansdale had called that afternoon to say that by all the signs in the zodiac a buyer was at hand. Pretty quick work, thought Mr. Hackett, who slumbered contentedly in the country airs, while Mr. Blandings lay in torture on Manhattan Island, a hundred miles away, counting the minutes until he could stand again on the height of Bald Mountain and clutch it to him as a child clutches the Teddy bear without which life is not to be endured.

When the next Saturday finally came, Mr. and Mrs. Blandings were on Bald Mountain early. With the real-estate man they once again wandered among the scattered snake fences, the rusty, slack barbed wire, the slowly melting stone walls of the Old Hackett Property. "The owner said he'd be up this way sometime this morning," the real-estate man said, looking at his watch. From the vagueness of his utterance it was not to be gathered that he had delivered the most explicit instructions to Mr. Hackett the night before. "For God's sake don't get there a minute before half-past eleven, Eph," he had emphasized. "I want them to be restless."

While they trod the springy, water-bearing earth of the warm mountainside, the Blandings found new fascinations in the old Hackett place. They counted the barns across the road like auditors checking a voucher list; indeed, there were four barns, just as the advertisement had said. There was what had been a cow barn; the remains of a horse barn; a structure that could have been called a carriage shed except for the big hayloft that made its second story. Then there was something that the real-estate man referred to as "the calf barn," in which there was a fascinating rope-and-wheel arrangement whereby the Hackett men had apparently hoisted their beef cattle up by the hoofs for the sledge blow that preceded slaughter. Not mentioned in the advertisement, and not noticed by the Blandings in the first fever of their glances a week ago, was a chicken house, the remains of what must once have been a pigpen, two small hay barns, and a generous collection of privies.

“I must say,” said Mrs. Blandings, thinking of the warm, sunlit pictures full of the order and prosperity of the 1890’s she had seen on the living-room walls the week before, “I must say it all seems rather terribly ramshackle.”

The real-estate man smiled. “You’ve got to be able to visualize,” he said.

There was no more talk about order or repair. The real-estate man’s remark had been genial and straightforward, but it was a rebuke, the Blandings felt, and a deserved one.

The conversation shifted from the works of man to those of God. In the week that had gone by since the Blandings’ first visit, the apple trees, neatly ranged in the orchard, had bedecked themselves like brides in their enchanting bloom. Mrs. Blandings, who had been cramming on the works of John James Audubon, spotted an oriole, a scarlet tanager, a blue-throated warbler; so many varieties of bird life, in fact, that she and Mr. Blandings lost all reverence for the dozens of robins that filled the air with their sweet, vernal song. It was still too early for the burst of wildflowers that was now obviously poised for the early days of summer, but violets were wild in the fields, lilies-of-the-valley dipped and nodded in the shady places, and clumps of wild flag sprang out of the swampy, rock-strewn land below the barns. By the time Mr. Hackett put in an appearance, driving a surprisingly large, glossy

Buick for the country bumpkin the Blandings had expected, the prospective purchasers were drunk on the sights and sounds of spring on Bald Mountain.

The interview with Mr. Hackett fell notably short of decisiveness. Mr. Blandings, hearing him constantly referred to as the Hackett "son," was not prepared to find a man aged between fifty-five and sixty. He had expected him, also, to be taciturn, as befitted a Nutmeg Yankee, and he was thrown off his stride to find him endlessly garrulous. The Hackett conversation, however, did not cohere; it was vacuous and shrewd, vague and incisive, by bewildering and unpredictable turns. Mr. Blandings almost immediately discovered that he did not know on what level the conversation should be pitched, nor even with what assumptions it should begin. He felt, somehow, that to announce himself in so many words as a possible purchaser of Mr. Hackett's property was to commit a diplomatic fault that would put him on the defensive and cost him money; he inclined, therefore, to discuss the rich arborology of the Hackett land as a substitute topic. Of this, Mr. Hackett appeared to be not particularly conscious, one way or another; for his part he seemed unable to concentrate on anything except Franklin Delano Roosevelt. The two topics had few points of tangency—but lumber was one of them, for Mr. Hackett, after his father's death, had left Bald Mountain to establish a small feed store and lumberyard in the little town in the valley beneath them, and attributed his small margin of profit directly and violently to the occupant of the White House. Although the matter of house and land purchase was yet to be raised, Mr. Hackett would periodically haul the conversation around to the extremely favorable prices he not only *could* give to Mr. Blandings but *would* give him, that very afternoon, if Mr. Blandings could state without delay what quantities of what grades of building lumber he would be requiring. Mrs. Blandings, seeing her husband baffled, attempted to use Mr. Hackett's boyhood and young manhood on Bald Mountain as conversational gambits, and by drawing him out on these formative years to get the subject on the track of possible title negotiation. Mr. Hackett appeared to have no reminiscences whatsoever, except of occasional visits made to Schenectady, New York, and these Mrs. Blandings could not incorporate in her plan. The real-estate man, from long, successful experience, said nothing; he was in effect the farm hand supervising a barnyard mating; if the parties to it were momentarily coy, coercion was worse than useless; it was inevitable that at some point soon forces stronger and more violent than anything within his control would take over and carry matters to their inevitable conclusion. He had seen the process too often to be impatient of the seemingly aimless preliminaries.

The Blandings ended an hour's tour with Mr. Hackett, breathless but frustrated. It had successively but obscurely appeared that Mr. Hackett would not sell any of his property on Bald Mountain at any price; that he would sell part but not all, and only under incomprehensible circumstances; that he was open to any reasonable offer; and that he was unaware that any matter of sale was under discussion. His desire to sell building materials to the Blandings, as well as an extensive line of agricultural machinery to which he began alluding later, was, however, not only clear but urgent. When he finally got into his shiny Buick to drive away, everything was much higher up in the air than before his arrival. He parted from the Blandings with a maddening reference to the necessity they would be under of cleaning out an old well into which he had fallen at the age of seven, he said, and for which he would like to provide them with a new bucket chain the following week at the wholesale price.

As his car vanished down the hill the Blandings looked about for the real-estate man. They discovered him some distance away, throwing rocks at a dead cherry tree. Only then did they realize that he had wandered off perhaps twenty minutes before.

"Well," he said cheerfully, "did you get down to business?"

"Well," said Mr. Blandings, "in one way we—"

"No they didn't," said Mrs. Blandings, crisply. "Men complain about women talking and then they—"

"Tell you what," said the real-estate man. "Eph Hackett is going to want an offer. A definite offer. If you think you can wait for him to commit himself you'll wait a century. But there's going to be a lot of real-estate activity up this way this year, by all the signs, and sooner or later somebody is going to come along and give him just about what he wants for this property. If you good people are seriously interested in it, my advice is to speak for it."

He looked at his watch. "I'm going to have to excuse myself in another couple of minutes," he said. "Some other people are coming up on the afternoon train, and I promised I'd meet them. They seem to have got wind of this place and they said they just sort of wanted to come up and look around."

Deep, black panic filled the souls of Mr. and Mrs. Blandings. These hateful Other People, nonexistent until that second, were instantly bodied forth in three glaring and hideous dimensions. They were shrewd, sharp, and predatory; they would assay the Hackett acres in a flash, make a curt offer, and be instantly accepted.

Then they would tear down the old house and erect a suburban villa, with dormers, fake half-timbering, and a varicolored asbestos-shingle roof on the ravished foundations of the immemorial Hackett manor. Mrs. Blandings wanted to cry but was too frightened. Mr. Blandings smiled a smile at the real-estate man that had all the insouciance of a sex fiend in the police line-up; a misshapen, terrible thing.

"Thanks for all your time and trouble," he twisted his mouth to say. "We'll think things over and write you from New York."

Never in his life had Mr. Blandings worked so hard on a piece of advertising copy as he now worked on the letter to the real-estate man; something that would convey to that deft practitioner the precise blend of active arousal, cool disinterest, "ability to visualize," and refusal to be carried away by daydreams that Mr. Blandings felt was called for. And never had Mr. Blandings had so much trouble with a client as he now had with his wife.

For one thing, all consideration of the letter as a work of art had three separate times to be postponed while a vast soul struggle went on to re-examine a question that had already been solemnly decided: was a place in the country something the Blandings really *had* to have, after a married lifetime of fifteen years in which, until six weeks ago, no lack of real estate had been felt? The process always brought forth the same answer, but never by the same route. What proved to be the final decision was arrived at via the Blandings' children, concerning whom, Mrs. Blandings now admitted, both parents had been somewhat thoughtless.

Ever since the Blandings' daughters had outgrown their little days of pail-and-shovel happiness at the seashore, the Blandings had packed them off, without much ceremony, for summers at Camp Mahottapottawamagog; they would be due, indeed, to take off for this New England paradise again in a very few weeks, to stay until it was almost time for the progressive school by the asphalt works to reopen its enlightened doors in September. The girls had always come home after Labor Day lithe and brown, but it was not the most considerate way to treat your own flesh and blood, Mr. and Mrs. Blandings agreed, particularly now that adolescence had begun for one and was an imminent prospect for the other. Girls needed their parents at this life juncture as they had seldom needed them before; if the ties of intimacy had been frayed by the headlong, heedless life of parents-on-the-make in the city, what else could so sweetly knit them up as a home in the country which would become the family foundation for all the years to come? Young men would be entering their daughters' lives in a year or two; it could almost be said that there was not a minute to lose.

Mr. Blandings briefly traced the doleful state of civilization and society to the loss of authority and respect vested in the family relationship. Then he figured on the back of an envelope for a minute and announced that the elimination of summer camp, once a country home made it superfluous, would amount to an annual saving of better than $1000. The way one got ahead in the world was to *invest* one's money in the substantial things of life; where the Blandings had obviously been shortsighted was in letting Mr. Blandings' pleasantly comfortable income be frittered away in mere *expenditures* which vanished, leaving no residue of permanence behind them. The business of summer camps was a perfect case in point.

The Blandings' daughters, Betsy and Joan, took the news of a possible country home with an appalling calm. At thirteen, Betsy was finding her teeth braces a tragic hobble to approaching womanhood; Joan, at eleven, was a soberly intellectual child who appeared to be anxious to pick up as soon as possible from where Madame Curie had some years earlier been forced to leave off. Mr. Blandings loved his daughters, but he sorely missed the gurgling and affectionate childhood during which they had both regarded him as God, and fought bloodily for his lightest favor; there was certainly not much fun in his daughters these days, he reflected, hoping that sometime soon an emotional linkage from them to him would again become apparent. At present, it was obvious that both of them regarded him as a husk.

"Miss Stellwagon says that anybody who remodels an old colonial house in these modern times is no better than a dupe," said Betsy. "Is this a colonial house?"

"It is in a sort of a way," said Mr. Blandings.

"Miss Stellwagon says that sort of thing is a form of totem worship," said Betsy.

"I am not asking for Miss Stellwagon's opinions," said Mr. Blandings, "tell your crackpot heroine with my compliments."

"There isn't any use sending the children to an expensive school and then undermining a teacher's authority in the parents' living room," said Mrs. Blandings.

"I'm not undermining anybody," said Mr. Blandings. "I just get so damn tired of hearing this woman's pronouncements. Stellwagon on Housing, Stellwagon on Isotopes, Stellwagon on the Holy Ghost, Stellwagon on—"

"I want to live in a Dymaxion house," said Joan. "It's built on a mast like a tent and it revolves with the sun. When it wears out you throw it away and get another one."

"I won't go picking blueberries and churning

butter in any old country house," said Betsy. "We read about the division of labor last week. Shopping at the Supermarket is the most efficient way to—"

"Or if it isn't a Dymaxion it could be a Stout Mobile Home," said Joan. "It comes all folded up, and when you find a place you like you unfold it and plug in for water and electricity, and when you get tired there you fold it up and find someplace else. When a new model comes out you trade your old one in like a used car."

"Don't you kids want to live in something permanent and substantial?" asked Mr. Blandings. "Do you just want to live in upper berths and merry-go-rounds? This house we're talking about was built before this country became a nation. It has dignity."

"How gruesome!" said Betsy.

"Maybe we could hitch a Zamboni Power Unit onto it," said Joan. "It's the kitchen and bathrooms and heating unit and power generator all rolled up into the size of a refrigerator. You fasten it onto any old house, just the way you fasten a locomotive onto any old freight train, and *zip*—it makes the house *work*. They're going to start building them year after next. I read it."

"You'd have rooms of your own," said Mrs. Blandings, a touch of wheedling in her voice. "Nice big rooms that you could furnish and decorate yourselves, the way you liked best."

"Partitions in a house are obsolete," said Betsy. "An enlightened house has no interior walls—only screens you can move about at will, Miss Stellwagon says. Mother, won't you please ask Dr. Shields to take these torture things off my teeth before the Commencement dance next week?"

"It's past bedtime for both of you," said Mrs. Blandings. "If we lived in the country, someday we could have a tennis court and a swimming pool, maybe."

The children brightened perceptibly. Betsy had somehow learned to play one of the best games of thirteen-year-old tennis Mr. Blandings had ever seen; Joan's prowess lay in swimming under water; she had developed such a lung reserve that she seldom appeared back on the surface of a swimming pool until between eighty-five and a hundred seconds after she had dived into it. The few times Mrs. Blandings had been privileged to see this exhibition she had almost fainted of anxiety.

"That would be more like it," the two said in unison. They retired without protest and without further allusions to any subject except dentistry.

"The children will love it when they *see* it," said Mrs. Blandings, as soon as she and her husband were alone.

"The way they talked made me realize how much they need a place like Bald Mountain," said Mr. Blandings, soberly. "Our generation is a failure with its children. A fifteen-foot horizontal slice in a New York apartment house—it's preposterous to call a slab like that a *home* where kids can get any sort of reality out of their relationship to nature and society—or even their own parents."

"Joan could have a laboratory in the cellar if she's really set on being a physical chemist," said Mrs. Blandings. "Do you suppose she really will be?"

Mr. Blandings did not answer. A dreamy look had come into his eye. "This is something we should do for the children, even if we disregarded ourselves," he said.

The basic question being at last resolved on a high plane, there remained the problem, almost as weighty, of what to offer in the way of money for the Old Hackett Property. It had appeared that Mr. Hackett was "asking" $15,000. So the real-estate man had said, anyway—but had he not also said that Mr. Hackett might be persuaded to take less, or even "a whole lot less"? How much *was* "a whole lot less"? Where did an offer cease to be shrewd and become merely insulting? Mr. Blandings had few landmarks in these woods, save that on the occasions when he had felt it decorous to talk money with the real-estate man, an easy, round, vague figure of $10,000 had now and again cropped up. This was not, of course, referable to any one piece of property anywhere, and least of all the old Hackett place—or was that precisely what the real-estate man was trying to say in a necessarily elliptical fashion? Among his friends and acquaintances, Mr. Blandings could not discover a soul who had ever paid that sum for anything: his friends had paid either $2500 for a few acres and an old barn or $75,000 for a ready-made estate. There seemed to be no transactions in between.

The letter that Mr. Blandings finally mailed, with the grudging approval of his wife, was a seventeenth draft, in which every word had been weighed and tested.

"My wife and I," he wrote, "have been considering an offer we might feel disposed to make for the property described as the 'old Hackett place' which we have several times had the pleasure of visiting with you. After due consideration I arrive at a value to me, for the property as it stands, of $9000. I am accordingly glad to propose a cash payment of $4500 and the assumption of a first mortgage which Mr. Hackett would hold to a like amount. If you will convey this proposal to the owner and let me have word at your convenience, I shall be much obliged."

Mr. Blandings considered this letter a masterpiece as he read it over one final time. It was curt but friendly, businesslike but open. It had a genial take-it-or-leave-it quality that could scarcely fail to impress itself on the real-estate man and old Ephemus Hackett both. In picking the $9000 figure Mr. Blandings had, of course, placed himself heavily on the defensive with his wife, who was sure it was too low and would merely serve as an invitation to Mr. Hackett to dispose of his homestead instantly to the Other People, who were still haunting her day and night. Mr. Blandings was equally haunted, but his position as a member of the male sex did not permit so unshackled a display of his fears.

The Blandings waited, twitching, for a response from the real-estate man. When, after an eon of seventy-two hours, it came, Mr. Blandings ripped open the envelope and read, sweatily, the blunt first paragraph:

"Dear Mr. Blandings: I have conveyed your offer to Mr. Hackett and I am sorry to say that he is not interested. . . ."

The Blandings swam in a red mist of despair, but somehow read on:

"Although I would not presume to set my own figure on the worth of what we have discussed as the Hackett property, I hope you will not think me forward if I suggest that in my opinion you have somewhat undervalued it. The old house has a definite antique value, and this is something that is bound to increase. I know of no view more superb in all the state than that which the property commands, and it is most unusual to find such a view combined with a brook of the size that happens to run through the upper fields we bounded. The value of the oak grove to the south cannot be discounted, either; this is first-growth timber and I can assure you out of my own familiarity with many acres in the county that it is somewhat unique. Although you have an unusual seclusion at the top of the mountain, you happen to be close to not one but two arterial highways, and the property is likewise halfway distant between the stations of two railroad systems. I do not want my own enthusiasms to influence you, but if you see your way clear to making a revised offer, I think I can present it in such a way as to recapture Mr. Hackett's consideration.

"For your own protection I should point out that your letter did not mention any definite acreage to which your offer applied. The Hackett family has always owned a very considerable amount of land on or near Bald Mountain, but I assumed that your interest applied to 'the fifty acres, more or less,' to which we alluded in our discussions and confined most of our attention on your several pleasant visits."

Disappointment, relief, and chagrin pursued one another through Mr. Blandings' vitals. The disappointment in the real-estate man's first two lines was vastly mitigated by the suggestion in the rest of his letter that the way was still open to Mr. Hackett; the Other People, apparently, had not yet pre-empted everything. But if Mr. Blandings was relieved that the property still existed for him, he was mortified at the real-estate man's sharp remark about the acreage. Mr. Hackett's theological vagueness about just what fields out of his inheritance he was actually proposing to convey had left Mr. Blandings baffled, and after a little while he had ceased to ask questions about the exact boundaries, through the understandable emotion of not wanting to appear such a total fool to the real-estate man as not to be certain just what it was he had said he might be interested in buying. But now, if he felt chagrined, he also felt instructed. Fifty acres. Certainly. That was really what he had had in mind all along.

Mr. Blandings spent the next two days writing another eight-line letter to the real-estate man. With various rhetorical cuff shootings and throat clearings, he raised his offer to $10,500, of which $5500 would be cash, and said that yes of course he had been talking about the fifty acres that seemed to form more or less the epicenter of Mr. Hackett's domain. He mailed it after another day's delay to indicate the casual quality of his interest in the whole business, and lay sleepless each night until the answer came. Mr. Hackett, the real-estate man then reported, had given this offer a more favorable consideration than the first but, after deliberation, had declined it.

That was all. No selling, no come-on stuff, no

nothing. Obviously the real-estate man had lost interest in the whole proceeding. The hideous specter of the Other People rose up to torture the Blandings now more frightfully than ever. The man was a coarse, loud creature with an Elk's tooth on his watch chain; the woman was a shrill bitch with ebony-tinted lips and fingernails. The property was theirs for certain, spirited out from under the Blandings' noses during a haggle over a few miserable pennies. Roweled by these nightmares, Mr. Blandings raised his ante to $11,000 in a letter that said, with a finality that made his hand shake as he signed it, that this was the last.

Utter silence ensued.

It was a Tuesday morning of a week later when Mr. Blandings' office phone rang and the real-estate man's voice came from the receiver. He gripped the desk and prepared for the blow that would crush him.

"I think I have good news for you," the real-estate man said. Mr. Blandings' vasomotor system relaxed and blood flowed again in his smaller capillaries. "Mr. Hackett says he'll accept that $11,000 proposition, provided it's net."

Mr. Blandings was instantly wafted from an office on the fiftieth floor of a New York skyscraper to a position a little lower than the angels, but not much. In the midst of his transport

Mr. Blandings was wafted from an office in a New York skyscraper to a position a little lower than the angels, but not much.

he managed to say “Fine” in what he hoped was a voice of minimum inflection. He was still afraid of betraying something to somebody; what or whom he did not know. But he did forget his pose of inscrutability enough to say, with the first frankness that had characterized him since he saw the Hackett acres, “What do you mean by ‘provided it’s net’?”

“That you pay the commission,” said the real-estate man patiently. “It’s five per cent, you know.”

With no more pause than the Elder Morgan sweeping aside a quibble involved in the creation of United States Steel, Mr. Blandings gave a noise of assent. He even made a remark about “not letting a little thing like that stand between us.” What was five per cent?

“Good,” said the real-estate man. His computation, made five weeks before as the Blandings stood beside the fireplaces in the cellar of the old Hackett house had turned out well within the limit-of-error he was in the habit of setting for himself.

III
The Deed

Mrs. Blandings sat under the drier at the hairdressing establishment of Vincent & Henri and dreamed a dream. The children had been successfully packed off to camp, and she had some time, now, for fancies. The Old Hackett Property was securely hers and her husband's at last. No papers had yet been exchanged, but verbal assurances were enough to make it certain that the Other People had been vanquished. They must slink off now to acquire elsewhere some portion of the submarginal land that comprised the rest of the continental United States: the perfection of the Hackett acres could never be theirs. Mrs. Blandings relaxed and felt generous toward them—even a bit ashamed of the venomous hatred that had shaken her toward people she had never seen, whose name she did not even know. But with them happily out of her way she could direct her thoughts into the clear, unobstructed channels of creation—the creation, on the top of Bald Mountain, of enchantment simple and enchantment pure. The stone walls would be rebuilt, firm and square. The snake fences would be put to rights and gleam with whitewash. The drooping barns would become again what they had been in the photographs that attested to their handsome, square-shouldered past. The orchards would be pruned and sprayed and tidied; the grove of magnificent oak trees cleared of its dead branches and fallen trunks; the brook cleaned, to glint and ripple among its stones. Around the old house would be a velvet lawn, and in beds and pockets and artful places she would plant such ingenious combinations of bulbs, rhizomes, tubers, shrubs, slips, bushes, and seedlings that, from the first yellow crocus in the spring to the last purple aster of the waning autumn, the Blandings' place atop Bald Mountain would be a glowing altarpiece of flowers. She and her husband and the children would bloom with country health, fed on country milk, country eggs, country butter. Inside the old house, the floors would glitter and the chintzes rustle, and there would be a deep and beautiful and solid peace. . . .

Impatience suddenly curdled in Mrs. Blandings. It would be *weeks* before she could begin this new life to which she had dedicated herself. Her husband and Mr. Hackett had first to sign a purchase agreement; then, after an infinite hocus-pocus that would involve her husband's young friend and attorney, Bill Cole, Mr. Hackett, and heaven knew who all else, the deed would be signed in the Lansdale County Courthouse and the property "conveyed." It was tedious beyond belief.

Meanwhile, Bald Mountain was deteriorating day by day, it was only too obvious. She had seen, for example, half a dozen disgusting bowers of tent caterpillars, their dirty, gray veils draped in the V's of the lovely apple trees in her orchard. This had been aesthetically displeasing when she had first seen them, but now it was a disaster; these were *her* trees the caterpillars were slowly munching. God knew what other insect depredations were going on here, there, and elsewhere, totally unknown to her, Mrs. Blandings reflected with rising dismay; the acres would have to be gone over, leaf by leaf, stick by stick, like a well-kept terrace. What dancing leaf would next be chewed by what beetle; what regal wild lily next be engulfed by what straying cow; what horrid worms would bore into what sweet fruit, Mrs. Blandings did not know, but found it all too easy to imagine. She had ached for land of her own to end the gnawing insecurity of the city dweller, far removed from the roots of subsistence; she had flung herself for protection on the sweet bosom of the earth and suddenly she was chill and damp and crawling with its vermin.

A cloud passed over the sun, and through the hairdressers' window Mrs. Blandings saw the cement sidewalks of the city turn from gold to gray. Heavens, she thought, it might *rain!* If it rained hard enough the lovely soil for her gardens would most certainly wash down to the swamp in

She had flung herself on the sweet bosom of the earth and suddenly she was chill and damp and crawling with its vermin.

which the brook rose; it would then sluice down Bald Mountain to the river and be carried by the river to the sea. In a flash, Bald Mountain was eroded to the rocks, and the Blandings stood naked, starving, and alone. Mrs. Blandings shuddered and quickly sought a comforting image. Bald Mountain had, after all, endured geological epochs of disaster upon disaster, and still emerged to be the flower-strewn, haze-enveloped enchantment her eyes had first encountered only a few weeks ago. Perhaps, then, it would survive one more shower without dissolution—but it was hard not to worry, really very hard indeed. Mrs. Blandings tried to envision the planet, still round, still revolving, still the flowering earth after the millions of years of hail and ice and flood and hurricane it had endured since the Creation, and presently she felt a little better and fell to work imagining cretonnes.

When Mr. Blandings came home that evening he was grumpy. He criticized his wife's new hair-do, but otherwise had no conversation in him until the end of the second cocktail. Then it came out that the real-estate man had called him on the telephone that afternoon to say that "apparently Mr. Hackett has been a little overoptimistic about the acreage"; it was probably going to survey closer to thirty-five acres than fifty.

"It" had continued to be a portion of the earth's surface indicated by Mr. Hackett's sweeping gestures, later somewhat more closely defined by a walk the Blandings had taken with him through thickets, swamps, and fields, following the course of a puzzling alternation of walls, fences, scrub trees, and brush. It had seemed like a good, generous tract of land to Mr. Blandings, and since he and the real-estate man had always talked about "fifty acres" in the same sort of take-it-for-granted way they would have used in discussing a pound of tea, Mr. Blandings had assumed that the two were one and the same. Now he had been made sharply aware that they were not, and that nobody had ever said they were; he was the victim of self-hypnosis, and he was consequently vexed with his wife. He suddenly remembered the letter with which the real-estate man had responded to his $9000 offer, and left his third cocktail untasted while he rooted it out from the pile of papers on his desk; his cheeks flushed as he saw the words "fifty acres, more or less" carefully set down inside quotation marks. The fifty acres, then, had been a figure of speech. He should have known.

Mr. Blandings' third cocktail mellowed his judgments a little; he was surprised and relieved when Mrs. Blandings pooh-poohed the importance of the whole thing and admitted she would actually be happier with thirty-five acres than with fifty. She had been thinking hard about tent caterpillars, cutworms, Japanese beetles, locusts, soil erosion, hurricanes, and floods, and was swiftly coming to regard acreage as a measure more of responsibility than of possession. "I don't know what we'd do with any more acres anyway," she said.

Mr. Blandings drained a final goblet at one draft, and the cosmos suddenly rearranged itself in more agreeable proportions.

"Thirty-five acres still lots acres," Mr. Blandings agreed buoyantly, as he rounded a chair that had interposed itself between him and the dining room.

• • •

"You're being flimflammed," said Bill Cole, Mr. Blandings' young attorney. He leaned across Mr. Blandings' office desk and gestured earnestly with his silver pencil. "I don't get all the ins and outs of this business yet, but I don't like a client of mine to enter a verbal agreement to buy fifty acres and then have it turn out that he's going to buy thirty-five acres for the same price. I'm all in favor of going to this Hackett-whoever-he-is and telling him the whole deal's off."

Mr. Blandings' blood turned icy cold. It was one thing to retain a friend to give you sound legal advice on deeds and purchase contracts; it was another thing for that friend to become intrusive in one's personal affairs.

"No," he said. Just when he thought things were really settled and the Hackett property his to have and hold forever, here was the whole miserable business drifting loose from its moorings all over again. "I couldn't possibly do that. I'm committed and I'm perfectly glad to be committed. I've told them to draw up a purchase agreement for thirty-five acres."

"What are you asking my advice for, then?" said Bill Cole. "And why do you always wait to call me in until you've gone and committed yourself to something and there's nothing for me to do except try to clean up behind you? Remember the time you bought that carload of butter two years ago?"

Mr. Blandings had no wish to be reminded of the occasion when he and another Banton & Dascomb copywriter had thought it a brilliant idea to take a margin flier on the Chicago Mercantile Exchange at a time when Mr. Blandings did not even know how to go about buying a government bond.

"That has nothing to do with our present topic," said Mr. Blandings.

"It is identical with our present topic," said Bill Cole. "I will write to this Hackett and tell him he can either kick in with those fifteen acres he's mislaid, reduce the price, or find another sucker."

"No," said Mr. Blandings, rigid in his chair. "Can't I make it clear to you that I *want* this property? It isn't just another chunk of real estate. It's something Muriel and I feel very deeply about. It's going to be our"—he swallowed suddenly—"home."

Bill Cole shrugged. "You've got to make some sort of stand," he said. "And you've *got* to have more land to go with that house and all those barns that Muriel is drooling about. Maybe you have all you think you need for protection now, but when the whole stinking thing comes up for resale someday, you'll find that you can get rid of the property much more advantageously if you have a decently sizable amount of land to offer."

How, Mr. Blandings thought to himself in a silent frenzy, can this young friend of mine be so colossally stupid? He graduated from the Harvard Law School in the top tenth of his class, he was a Rhodes Scholar after that, and now he's on his way to being head of the whole legal department of General Bag—and yet he can sit here and talk about "resale" and "disposal" and "getting rid of" what I have just been breaking my heart to acquire. Can't he *understand?*

"I don't want anything upset," he said aloud. "Muriel and I have found exactly what we want, and I don't see why that can't be that."

Bill Cole laid down the pencil with which he had been doing some scratch arithmetic.

"Have you any idea how much those brigands have traded you up already without your knowing that anything has happened to you?" he asked. "You offered $9000 for fifty acres the first time around, didn't you?"

Mr. Blandings nodded. The conversation was past the point where he dared admit to Bill Cole that he had forgotten to specify what acreage he was offering to buy with the $9000, and that the seller's agent had had to remind him.

"That's $180 an acre," said Bill Cole. "I won't comment on that except to remind you I know that part of the country as well as you do, and $100 is the standard top-gouge real-estate price per acre to city slickers. When the natives sell to one another it's at around $40 an acre or less. However, we'll accept your $180 an acre as par, and assume it represents a fair price for the acreage plus various unimproved structures."

"The house has a definite antique value that is bound to increase," said Mr. Blandings, in a stilted quotation of the real-estate man's letter.

"We'll waive the antique value," said Bill Cole. "If you discover a set of Governor Winthrop's false teeth in a chimney breast I will be the first to congratulate you. So you finally raised your offer to $11,000, which is $220 an acre. Then first they stick you for the commission, which brings you up to $231 an acre, and now they tell you that your money is only going to buy you thirty-five acres, which brings the price up to $330 an acre."

"When are you going to come to your point?" asked Mr. Blandings.

"*That* is my point," said Bill Cole. "This is an eighty-four per cent increase over your first offer, and a fifty per cent increase over what you said was your final offer, and far from protesting, you don't even seem to know that this has been going on."

"Look," said Mr. Blandings. "If you're criticizing me for not having bought the whole of Manhattan Island for $24 and a bottle of Holland gin, you're not affecting me. Muriel and I were lucky enough to find what I am not ashamed to call our Dream Property after six weeks on the kind of hunt that takes some people five years. So I snapped it up, before it got away from me. It takes us two and a half hours to get up there now, but someday soon they'll perfect the helicopter and then it'll be a twenty-five-minute hop from Grand Central, and values are going to skyrocket. I don't want to see Lansdale become a suburb, but I'll bet it will."

"Anybody been feeding you that?" Bill Cole asked sharply.

"No," said Mr. Blandings. "That's my own evaluation. I'm doing some constructive forecasting, that's all."

Bill Cole took off his reading glasses, and snapped the case on them.

"Look," he said. "Every time you get a little tight, you weep on my shoulder about what a terrible thing the advertising-agency business is for a sensitive soul like yourself because you make your living out of bamboozling the American public. I would say that a small part of this victimized group has now redressed the balance. Humanly, I am willing to leave it at that. As your attorney, however, I insist that a letter of record go to Hackett, *et al.,* in the matter of fifty acres versus thirty-five acres, and if it does not you can get some other lawyer to check your purchase contract and put the deeds through."

After another half-hour of discussion Mr. Blandings signed a considerably cooled-off version of the first scorching letter Bill Cole had composed. It emphasized that Mr. Blandings, having discussed the purchase of fifty acres, wished to purchase fifty acres. He mailed it that evening and, in alternations of depression and anxiety, waited for a reply.

"Mr. Hackett is nonplused," the real-estate man wrote him with chilly decorum several days later, "to have a new proposition put before him at the instance of your lawyer just when the original one was about to be ratified. It is, perhaps, unfortunate that Mr. Hackett's original estimate of the acreage turned out to be overgenerous, but subsequent to your offer he has had several other tempting proposals and has asked that I tell you he would be agreeable to the cancellation of any verbal agreements between you and him, should you have any feeling of dissatisfaction with the representations made."

Mr. Blandings spent a day cursing Bill Cole to the ulterior depths of nether hell. Bill had jeopardized his purchase of the Old Hackett Property. This was bad enough, but this Mr. Blandings could, and instantly did, retrieve by dispatching a letter of cordial disacknowledgment for what he had written at Bill's urging. But Bill had also planted in Mr. Blandings' mind the cancerous seed of suspicion, now growing to a certainty, that he *was* being flimflammed. He was being flimflammed and there was nothing he could do about it because he would rather be flimflammed and get the Hackett property than not be flimflammed and not get it. Mr. Hackett had looked him coolly up and down and taken his measure, for once, for all. Mr. Blandings would never admit to Bill Cole, or to his wife, that he had been so deftly frisked by an old windbag who gave the appearance of being unable to keep his mind on any one subject for more than thirty seconds, but in his heart he knew it to be so.

He sat in his living-room chair and brooded. Probably a very good thing, he slowly began to think, after his anger had run its course; probably a blessing in disguise. Once bitten, twice shy. Caution one must have in this complex business of buying and selling, and caution he had now acquired. This little going-over would stand him in good stead as the days of full ownership responsibility came upon him; it would not be long before he could smile at it, and perhaps even make a knowing jest at his own expense when, as a grizzled veteran of realty values, he would discuss his onetime innocence with the real-estate man. But caution, always, henceforth.

His musing was interrupted by his wife's voice from across the apartment sitting room.

"I wonder if we could make the calf barn into a guest house?" asked Mrs. Blandings.

"Why not?" said Mr. Blandings.

• • •

"Thirty-five acres, more or less—" That was what the purchase agreement, somewhat sulkily checked by Bill Cole, now told Mr. Blandings he was contracting to buy. That invariable suffix to mensuration, the "more-or-less" phrase, bothered Mr. Blandings as he saw it embedded in the formal agreement, but he no longer felt in a moral position to share his uncertainty with Bill Cole. He supposed, however, that it was a convention of legal phraseology and had only the same sort of significance as the other phrase in the agreement which constantly referred to the location of the Hackett property as "Bald Mountain, *so called.*" A small, neat sketch map on tissue paper, traced from an aerial photograph, served, after all, to define the property without words. It had comforted Mr. Blandings to know that the property had to be surveyed with rod and transit and an official map made a part of the final papers, even though it had come to him as a surprise that the buyer, not the seller, was the one who bore the cost. However, he had cheerfully ponied up the $65 which met the bill of Mr. Henry Bintle, the local surveyor, and now he had before him the crisp blueprint of his boundaries that this outlay had just brought through the mails. He was to journey to the Lansdale County Seat with Bill Cole tomorrow for the ceremonies that would at last transform the Old Hackett

Property into the Old Blandings Property, and now he studied Mr. Bintle's blueprint and three pages of close-typed description of how the boundaries ran. He felt a sense of calm and security as he saw his own name an integral part of the map; the surveyor's jargon made a soothing singsong in his ear: ". . . thence along said stonewall fence forming the East boundary of said Lansdale Road, N 20° 27' E, 21.84 feet to the end of said stonewall fence, thence along a wire fence N 16° 31' W, 78.66 feet to a twenty-inch chestnut tree, thence in a straight line . . . stonewall fence . . . said boundary . . . thence westward . . . to a total of thirty-one and one-half acres as certified by me this twelfth day of June in the year of our Lord One Thousand Nine Hundred and—"

"To a total of *what?*" Mr. Blandings cried aloud.

He stared at the survey sheet without affecting in the slightest the figure of thirty-one and one-half acres as attested by Mr. Henry Bintle.

Fortunately for his bursting indignation, Bill Cole's number answered the moment he dialed it.

"Fascinating," said Bill Cole after Mr. Blandings had vented his first preliminary gasps.

"He can't *do* this," said Mr. Blandings.

"You have agreed to buy property as described by what is called metes and bounds," said Bill Cole, in an infuriating, flat voice of legal didacticism. "The sketch map with the purchase agreement controls a description of the area Hackett is selling and you are buying, and the survey map confirms this officially. The time to fight about the acreage was when I wrote that letter that you first emasculated and then totally disacknowledged four days later. If the map shows something that turns out to be thirty-one and a half acres, then the fact that this same area is loosely described elsewhere as thirty-five acres 'more or less' has very little to do with anything."

"There must be *something* to do," said Mr. Blandings.

"Your friend Mr. Hackett has an eye like Joe DiMaggio, that's all," said Bill Cole, blandly continuing. "He has a remarkable grasp of common fractions, too. Ten per cent off from thirty-five acres is thirty-one and a half acres. I guess he did that just to be on the safe side. Here and there there's a rough convention that ten per cent is the maximum or minimum tolerance a court might regard as the limit of fair play on either side. He seems to have hit that right on the button—couldn't have done better on a lathe."

"You don't seem disposed to be very helpful," said Mr. Blandings.

"In my opinion you are well beyond the best powers of Elihu Root," said Bill Cole. "I studied your papers this morning and observed with interest that at the same time Mr. Hackett was signing a so-called agreement to sell you thirty-five acres 'more or less' he was entering the probate court for permission to sell you thirty acres 'more or less.' That makes his intention seem pretty clear to you and me, but meanwhile you had written to that real-estate chap telling him your lawyer was a bum and that you were quite agreeable to the reduction from the original estimate, and that what the sketch map offered was what you wanted to buy. There may be some sort of stink that could still be raised, but the legal facts are pretty obscure by now, in view of your letter—and I don't want to get a reputation for ambulance chasing when my client doesn't even know he's been run over."

"Well," said Mr. Blandings, "maybe—"

"I'm looking forward to meeting Mr. Hackett," said Bill Cole, in a tone that indicated the conversation could now close. "He isn't just getting a bonus of eighty-four per cent out of you, after all. As of this minute he is getting a bonus of 104 per cent, and this is the first faint yip of pain he's drawn so far. I'll see you at the train gate in the morning."

Mr. Blandings found little to say to Bill Cole the next morning as the train bore them northward to the Lansdale County Seat, and Bill Cole seemed content to read two newspapers and a long legal document without pressing Mr. Blandings for conversation. When the two of them entered the bare, echoing room that served old Probate Judge Lester Quarles as his chambers, Mr. Blandings suddenly found himself feeling awed and embarrassed. The Judge was brisk. The real-estate man carried himself with a strange sort of reverence. Mr. Blandings found it hard to forgive Bill Cole for the air of jauntiness which he assumed for the proceedings. He had been prepared to treat Mr. Hackett with a freezing hauteur, and was therefore deeply taken aback at the blaze of hostility in Mr. Hackett's eyes directed at *him.* Mr. Hackett's aged mother, there to affix a palsied signature to some necessary papers, contributed an occasional shower of tears which made Mr. Blandings feel like a criminal; this was, she made it evident without comprehensible words, the occasion which bore out of her life and into the hands of a callous and pomaded barbarian (Mr. Blandings had had a haircut which made him look unfortunately sleek) the home to which she had come on a bridal night now sixty years gone by; where she had born three sons and a daughter and reared them all; where she had watched the maples leaf and the lilac flower, spring after spring, spring after spring, since the days when the United States was a country newly made whole after the sundering of a civil war.

Mr. Blandings was angry and guilty and apologetic and harassed all at the same time.

Mr. Hackett's aged mother contributed a shower of tears that made Mr. Blandings feel like a criminal.

There was nothing for him to do except sign his name occasionally where Bill Cole told him to, and to stare uncomfortably about the room in the awkward silences while Judge Quarles and Bill Cole looked over one another's shoulders. Finally, the moment came when Mr. Blandings handed over to Judge Quarles his certified check for $5500. He sighed deeply. The Judge immediately demanded four other checks—for tax adjustment, interest on something or other, for the real-estate man's brokerage and the Judge's own legal fee. They made a tidy sum in themselves. Bill Cole assented, and when the old Judge had them all together he solemnly scrutinized the amounts and signatures, and then handed to Bill Cole documents which Mr. Blandings was later to identify as an Administrator's Deed, a Quitclaim Deed, a Certificate of Title, and a handful of miscellaneous receipts. It was done.

"Well," said Bill Cole to his shrinking client, "it's all yours now—subject, of course, to that mortgage for the other half of your $11,000 purchase price." Judge Quarles cleared his throat in a terminal manner. Old Mrs. Hackett, spurred by a final welling up of emotion, offered an obscure observation to Mr. Blandings; indistinct but obviously insulting. Her son shook hands with the Judge and the real-estate man, nodded curtly to Bill Cole and Mr. Blandings, and guided his weeping mother out of the room, Mr. Blandings' certified check crumpled in his big fist. A moment later, Mr. Blandings and his young attorney were blinking on the step of the courthouse in the bright noon sun of a flawless June day.

"That's that," said Bill Cole.

Mr. Blandings could not escape the conviction that he had done something sneaky and illicit. The real-estate man joined them for a moment on the top of the steps, shook hands solemnly, and disappeared.

As to a feast day, a Mardi gras, Mr. and Mrs. Blandings had looked forward to the day when they alone, without benefit of the real-estate man, Mr. Hackett, or any other hangers-on, would be able to visit the old Hackett place and call it their own; to clutch the sod and establish their ownership of it; to find a skulking trespasser and order him off the fraction of the earth that now they owned alone among God's creatures. "To have and to hold to him, the said Grantee, his heirs and assigns, to his and their own proper use and benefit forever"—those were the words of their deed, almost Biblically beautiful, the Blandings thought, and they intended that all persons should know. In a more irreverent mood, they would rip a peeling strip of yellowed wallpaper from the rock-hard plaster of the old house, just to show they could.

And now the day was here. The deeds, the "instruments," that certified Mr. Blandings as a country-estate owner, free of the thralldom of the city forever, lay carefully deposited in a safe-deposit box that he had hired in the Lansdale National Bank. Backed by their solid assurances, he felt gay to the point of song as he and his wife drove through the network of back-country roads that crisscrossed the happy hill and valley of Lansdale County; a shiny new station wagon attested his importance as a man who must journey seven miles to his railroad station. He had never driven this tangle of roads himself, but he had watched closely in the days when he was beholden to the practiced turns and counterturns of the real-estate man's snappy convertible roadster. Right turn at the green mailbox; bear left when you come to the milk-stand across from the bright-red barn; straight ahead past the old cemetery; a sharp, hairpin left when you came to the great bole of the bleached and fallen chestnut that lay at the top of the rise where you could see a distant steeple.

It seemed to Mr. Blandings that he was a long time in coming to the fallen chestnut, and a few minutes later it struck him that perhaps he had never before in his life seen the deserted farm past which, on his left, he was now traveling. When he suddenly came to a sign saying SHRUNKS MILLS 2 MI. his pleasure in life, love, marriage, children, work, and the worship of an Unseen Power all totally vanished. He was lost: *he had bought a place in the country for $11,550 and now he could not find it!*

"I think we're lost," said Mrs. Blandings. Her husband turned on her savagely, but discovered that he had no materials for a retort.

"Why do you always speed up when you've lost

He had bought a place in the country for $11,550 and now he could not find it.

your way?" Mrs. Blandings pursued in her see-how-reasonable-I-am voice. "You don't give me any time to look for signposts."

Twenty minutes later Mr. Blandings gave up his ghastly show of sufficiency and spread his humiliation on the record; he stopped the station wagon and asked a lurching oaf on the roadway for directions. Mrs. Blandings gazed impassively through the windshield; she had been grossly insulted but she would maintain her ladyhood to the end. The roadside traveler had never heard of any such name as Hackett and knew nothing of a Hackett property but wondered if he could have a lift to Shrunks Mills, which apparently Mr. Blandings had again approached in a wide, sweeping, consistent circle.

Much later, Mr. Blandings got out of the station wagon and knocked on a farmhouse door. While hunting for Shrunks Mills, which had somehow escaped him along with everything else, he had suddenly come on the Lansdale railroad station, whence he had started two hours ago, bound for his seven-mile-distant home; having gone back to Shrunks Mills again to drop the wayfarer with whom he had become intimately entangled, he had returned to the Lansdale railroad station to start life anew for the third time. Not only could he not find his future home; he could not now find anything similar to what he had accidentally traversed before. "Excuse me," he said to a large woman with suds up to her elbows, "I wonder if you can tell me how close I am to the Old Hackett Property."

If he had displayed to his wife one tenth of the deference he now showed to this big, untidy, ferocious farm woman, she would have kissed and forgiven him in an instant. But a man could go just so far in self-abnegation, and no farther.

"Somebody's bought it," said the woman.

"I know," said Mr. Blandings. "That is, I—" He stopped, entrapped on the brink of a new disaster.

"Did *you* buy it?" asked the woman, coming to the heart of the matter with the instant perceptions of a woman who has lived all her life with animals.

A lie would do no good. A lie would make everything worse, if possible. The woman knew; her question was not a question. Mr. Blandings could feel himself turning the color of a new drainpipe.

"Yes," he said.

The woman's contralto laugh brought six children instantly to the sagging doorframe; six children and a hollow, saturnine man with a wry neck and a wad of tobacco in his cheek.

"So you're the fella Eph Hackett's unloaded his place on," the woman boomed. "And now you can't find it." She checked another echoing laugh. "Maybe you're lucky at that," she said.

Mr. Blandings detested her. He detested his wife. He detested himself. "Which way is it?" he asked, attempting to reject all other conversational gambits.

"Lord, mister," said the woman, "I don't know whether I can help you or not. I guess I never heard of anybody mislayin' where he lived, before. Or where he's goin' to live, anyway. You goin' to *farm* it?" she asked, her eyes like arrow tips.

"Just a little, I guess," said Mr. Blandings. He was wishing he had become a monk that time back in 1919 when an adolescent fit of religious fervor had hit him. With a vow of poverty, he would never have been able to write a $5500 check to anybody for anything; a vow of chastity would have precluded Mrs. Blandings and the Blandings children; a vow of obedience . . .

"Go ahead and try farming something 'just a little' around this country," said the woman. Her tone was not hostile; she was merely blustering him as she would have blustered one of her smaller children. "It'd do me good to get up at four o'clock in the morning 'just a little.' "

Suddenly she took pity on him. "Look," she said. "You want to get to Eph Hackett's place, I tell you what you better do. Go back to the Lansdale railroad station and ask somebody where Squantatuck Road is. Then . . ."

"What did she say?" asked Mrs. Blandings, with the correctness of a Prussian in a conquered city. Mr. Blandings, who, in his agony, had heard no word of the new directions, mumbled feebly and soon found himself again in Shrunks Mills, where his previous voyager, now leaning against a hardware-store window, regarded him with obvious relish.

It was near dusk when Mr. and Mrs. Blandings reached their home on Bald Mountain, so called. The project of clutching two handfuls of earth and holding them in a triumphant skyward V seemed no longer appropriate. The new owners watched as a murmuration of starlings swooped and chattered in the fading sky; from out a barn door the Blandings had never before noticed to be totally unhinged, a woodchuck the size of a collie half waddled, half slunk across the road. He cast a sneering look at the estranged couple, and faded into a tangle of brush. As if prodded by an invisible finger, a shingle high up on the old house roof broke loose from where it had lain since 1775 and slid with a scrambling noise down its fellows to the eaves, and there fell off. As the Blandings looked at the little scar of raw wood it had left behind, the top edge of the sun's red disk vanished behind the far, far distant Catskills.

IV

First Lamp of Architecture

Let's say your land'll cost you $10,000, round numbers," the real-estate man had occasionally said in the days before it had actually cost $11,550. "And let's say it'll cost you $10,000 to restore the old farmhouse. So you've made a $20,000 investment that'll stand you all the rest of your life, to say nothing of having a home to live in and the benefit of what your wife calls the 'indescribable charm of the place.' It's pretty hard to see how you're going to lose."

This lyric passage had served the Blandings in lieu of thought for several months until, one evening, Mrs. Blandings looked up from her mending.

"Do you suppose it's worth our while to remodel that old house?" she asked in a faraway voice.

If she had risen in church to confess the illegitimacy of the Blandings' daughters and ascribe each to a different father she could scarcely have had a more thunderous effect upon her husband.

"I only mean," she went on, in an effort to silence him, "that maybe somebody should look at it besides Mr. Funkhauser."

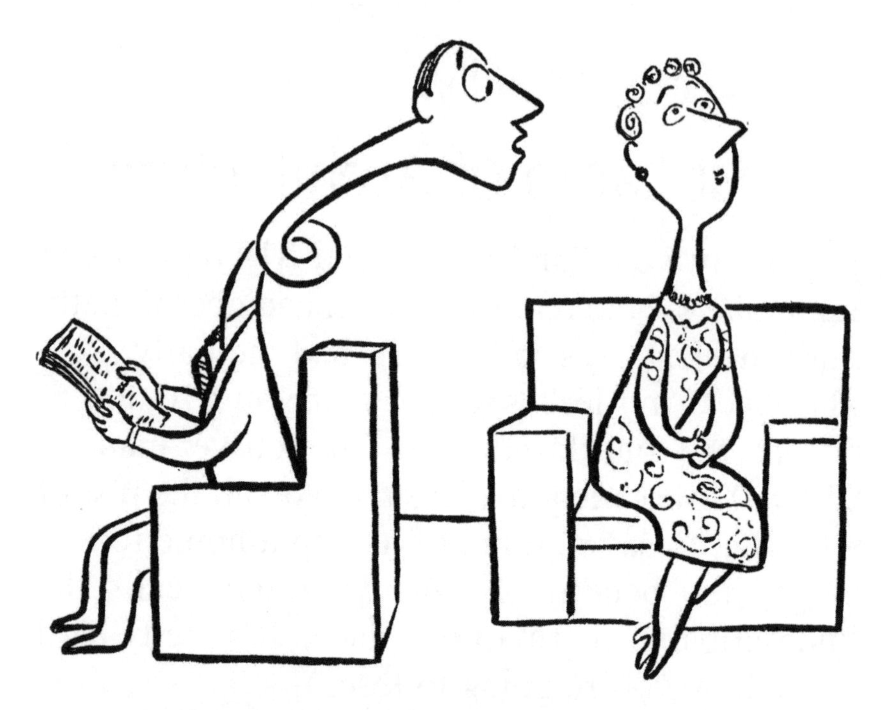

"Do you suppose it's worth our while to remodel that old house?" Mrs. Blandings asked in a faraway voice.

Mr. Funkhauser was a young architect who had done some farmhouse restoring for friends of the Blandings who, like them, had determined to make Lansdale County their country home. Mr. Blandings discovered that he had retained him during the course of a cocktail party at which the two had met for the first time. Mr. Funkhauser had been enchanted with the old Hackett house and pronounced it one of the truest gems of Revolutionary architecture he had ever seen—granted, of course, that the years of neglect and misunderstanding of its original purposes had taken their toll. By the time he had finished explaining to the Blandings where the original front door had been, the probable date of the addition of the ell, why the roof pitches of main house and ell were different, and where the original twelve-light windows had been replaced with double-hung sash, Mr. Blandings felt that his possible impulsive choice of an architect was well ratified by second sight. Working mostly from photographs plus some measurements taken one rainy day on Bald Mountain, Mr. Funkhauser had since been covering reams of sketch tissue with the graceful swashes of a 6-B pencil. The Blandings had found the results enchanting. "He's retained all the feeling of the old house," they would tell people, "in spite of all the changes. Look at the way he's blended that turret into the original lines. He really has an extraordinary instinct for what's right and what's wrong in that part of the countryside, and it's so remarkable he should have, coming from Brooklyn the way he does."

Mrs. Blandings' question seemed to alter this footing. Sensing trouble ahead, Mr. Blandings thrust out an immediate patrol.

"What's the matter with Funkhauser?" he demanded. "Last time I heard anything you were so crazy about his sketches you were practically getting into bed with him."

"I wish you could find some other expression to

"Mr. Funkhauser is so enthusiastic about everything that sometimes I think he gets carried away," said Mrs. Blandings.

indicate sympathy and understanding between two people," said Mrs. Blandings. "I only mean that Mr. Funkhauser is so enthusiastic about everything that sometimes I think he gets carried away, and I'd like to have some other sort of person take a look at the old house before we get too far along, just to make certain that it's going to keep on standing up, and things like that—an engineer, or somebody."

In no time Mr. Blandings came to believe that he himself had had this prudent idea. By now he once again felt sufficiently at ease with Bill Cole to consult with him, and it turned out that Bill Cole knew just the man—a good practical fellow who Bill Cole guaranteed would not be carried away by anything. It was arranged that as soon as he could find a day off, Mr. Fred Apollonio, construction engineer, would visit the Hackett property and give the Blandings the benefit of his most earthy advice.

Once, at three o'clock in the morning, it sleepily occurred to Mr. Blandings that if he was doing the right thing in calling upon Mr. Apollonio's experience, there must be some doubt whether he was doing it at the right time. He had bought his house and land for $11,550 and there were 31.5 acres of land, no more, no less; that was water over the dam. Since a city dweller could, as Bill Cole had emphasized, buy all the unencumbered land he wanted for $100 an acre, then it must be that the house had cost him the difference between $11,550 and $3150, or $8400, and he was now about to call a witness to testify that it might be worth—*nothing?* Mr. Blandings sat up sharply in bed, a thin band of sweat across his brow. But no, it would not be that. It would not. That noble old farmhouse that the stout young Hackett men of the Revolutionary days had hewn out of oak and ash and hickory and chestnut, the adz marks still sharp on the stout, inflexible beams . . .

Besides, it was unfair to make the house bear all

the burden of the difference between $11,550 and $3150, Mr. Blandings' thoughts continued. There were the barns; the barns and the shed and—and the privies, too, when you came to think of it. They were all worth something; quite a tidy sum, probably, if you wanted to sit down and tot everything up with a pencil. *No, they weren't, either,* said Mr. Blandings' daemon, in his ear. You damn well know they're not, Blandings; when it came to the question of fire insurance (which took you somewhat by surprise, by the way; you hadn't ever dreamed the rates would be that high when the real-estate man had suddenly turned insurance agent and asked to write your policies), you agreed that it wasn't worth while to insure the barns for a penny, and that $5000 was enough to carry on the old house. Why had you never before done the simple mental arithmetic of subtracting $3150 from $11,550? Why did you agree that the old house should be insured for $5000? That was the *one* sum most obviously wrong; either you should have set it up at $10,000 or $12,000, maybe, or else you shouldn't have put a penny on it. . . .

Mr. Blandings rose and groped for the bathroom. From the medicine cabinet he extracted a bottle of phenobarbital; he looked glumly for a minute at the red lettering on the label that said, CAUTION: MAY BE HABIT-FORMING, and swallowed two pellets.

• • •

Mr. Apollonio visited the old Hackett place with Mr. and Mrs. Blandings a week later. In his black shoes, dark business suit and derby, he made an odd picture among the roaming hills, particularly compared to Mr. Blandings in his slightly aggressive rural tweeds. But he was a mine of wisdom; Mr. Blandings marveled at the terms of easy familiarity on which he lived with every sort of structure: dams, bridges, tunnels, lofts, skyscrapers; even ships' hulls were matters of simple fact to him. He worked for the Port of New York Authority and had apparently been Assistant Chief of Rivet Design during the days of the building of the Great Bridge that now flung its exquisite steel shawl across the Hudson. Mr. Blandings felt a little silly at the idea of asking this master of stress-strain analysis, yield points, and rupture moduli to look at an old farmhouse of which nothing had ever been asked save that it should not blow off its hillside, but Mr. Apollonio set all at ease by a wave of his thick, stubby, competent hand. "Glad to pick up the extra money," he said, with simple candor.

On the site, Mr. Apollonio became wordless. Mrs. Blandings had expected him to bring a bag of instruments along, like a physician, and perhaps to practice the physician's rites of palpation and auscultation on her dwelling. But Mr. Apollonio's only instrument was a foot rule, parked in an especially tailored slot near his back pants pocket, and far from palpating her house, he did not even seem to want to go near it. He merely stood looking at it from about a hundred feet away, his hands on his hips, his derby pushed upward on his forehead. After five minutes of wordless contemplation, he went up to it and kicked it on one corner. Mr. and Mrs. Blandings winced in unison when something unidentified fell off.

Mr. Apollonio picked up the fragment, fumbled with it for a moment, and tossed it away. Then he opened the door through which Mr. and Mrs. Blandings had made their first ingress ever into their future home; when the door fell toward him as it had toward Mr. Blandings, Mr. Apollonio leaped aside as if he had encountered an African hartebeest. Mr. Blandings felt something give in the pit of his stomach when he reflected that this man who now recoiled from the cellar of their house was the same man who had regaled them on their upward train journey that morning with the tale of how he had stood on a plate atop the final girder for the western tower of the George Washington Bridge, in a thirty-five-mile wind.

Mr. Apollonio returned to his clients, dusting his hands, and spoke to them in a soft voice.

"You should ought to tear it down," he said.

Mr. Apollonio, whose competency was hard to question, went on to state his reasoning. "If your chimney was shot and your sills were O.K., I'd say go ahead, fix her up," said Mr. Apollonio. "If your sills were shot and your chimney was O.K. again I'd say go ahead, fix her up. But your sills are shot *and* your chimney is shot, so I say O.K., you better tear her down. You want a roof on your house? You won't have that one long, and if you did, you'd have to raise it a foot, foot 'n' a half, two foot, and cost you $2000 just for that—unless you want to keep Singer Midgets upstairs, maybe?"

His mellow laugh was a blasphemy in the everlasting hills.

"That stinking roughneck has simply no feeling for antiquity," said Mr. Blandings, taking a spastic gulp out of his glass.

"I wish you wouldn't drink when you're upset," said Mrs. Blandings. She and her husband were back in their city apartment again. The train trip home had been a trying journey, but Mr. Apollonio had not felt the blight in the air. He had been asked for a professional opinion and he had rendered it; his work done, he relaxed and talked cheerily about structural engineering all the weary way. "Standing on that bridge tower, now," he said, "before they threw the guide cable across the river to start the spinner working, I felt as safe as if I'd been in church. Safer. Boy, was it windy, though. I had to keep my two feet as close

Mr. Apollonio's mellow laugh was a blasphemy in the everlasting hills.

together 's if I'd been standing on a dime, and still I had to be braced against these gusts. Top of that girder must have whipped as much as an inch when one of them would hit it, but I'd designed every rivet in the whole pier, and I knew I was safe. She just hummed like a pipe organ, when the wind was steady.

"Friend of mine got crushed to death in an old barn up this way couple of years ago," he went on, his mood changing. "Looked as good as the day it was put up, for all anybody knew, but the termites had chewed the beams out hollow and one day when he went in there and tried to pull a hay rake out of the corner, the whole Goddamn thing just fell in on him." He shuddered. "Head smashed flatter'n a pancake when they pulled him out," he concluded, his happy face momentarily darkened.

It was not only to exorcise the picture of Mr. Apollonio's friend with his head squashed flatter than a pancake that Mr. Blandings now wished oblivion for the rest of the evening. The instant he entered his apartment he had written out a check for $50 to Mr. Apollonio's order, and dispatched it to him with a curt, correct note. Now Mr. Blandings was alone with God and Mrs. Blandings and there seemed no concealing from either of them that he had paid the not inconsiderable sum of $8400 for a structure which he had just been advised (for $50 more) to destroy. In Mr. Blandings' view his wife was an accessory before the fact and God stood convicted of the grossest sort of negligence—but condemn them as he might, he could see no recourse from either of them, or from the real-estate man or from Ephemus W. Hackett. The episode of the shrinking acreage had been one thing; he had elected to brush Bill Cole's protests aside and accept a *fait accompli.* But this was something else, and it was too much. Yet the real-estate man, Mr. Blandings' conscience perversely told him, had uttered not one slightest word of misrepresentation; had, in fact, done scarcely any of the "selling" that was associated with his tribe; had, in further fact, scarcely done anything at all except keep the channel clear for Mr. Blandings' own torrential, racing fantasies, and now and then supply them with a preposition or an adverb. As for Mr. Hackett, Mr. Blandings would like to fry him in hell—yet the record would show that Mr. Hackett had been a most reluctant seller, having rejected two offers and dictated the revision of a third before the purchase agreement was finally signed.

There remained, however, the luckless Mr. Funkhauser, still doodling happily on his sketch tissue, dreaming towers and battlements, spires and turrets, onto a lousy old wreck of a farmhouse that had neither sills nor chimney to support its own crumbling weight. Him, Mr. Blandings fired with a thunderclap suddenness that left, as one residue, a folder in the files of the American Institute of Architects labeled "Funkhauser-Blandings Grievance Case." After a chilly interchange of letters, and a consultation with Bill Cole on the Law of Contracts, Mr. Blandings gave up any attempt to wave aside Mr. Funkhauser's claim to a fee. He paid Mr. Funkhauser's bill of $435 for "Preliminary Plans for Restored Blandings Residence" and received the tracings and blueprints thereof.

Mr. Blandings fired Mr. Funkhauser with a thunderclap suddenness.

They were cold comfort. So was the report of Mr. Joe Perlasky, a local house wrecker and junk-yard proprietor whose extraordinarily neat piles of the dream wreckage of other days and other people lay on a corner of the little village at Bald Mountain's foot. Mr. Blandings had consulted him on the sly, in the hope of presenting to Mrs. Blandings the happy news that they could realize perhaps $2000 out of the materials salvaged from the razing of the structure that was to have been the home of their children's children. Mr. Perlasky, a stout little

Mr. Perlasky said he would take the house down, all neat and clean, and not charge a penny more than $950.

man with hands like frankfurters, had figured for fifteen minutes with an almost invisible pencil stub on the back of an old shirt cardboard and then announced that he would tear the house down, remove all materials, and leave everything neat and clean around the foundations and not charge Mr. Blandings a penny more than $950. *"Charge?"* cried Mr. Blandings. "'At's right," said Mr. Perlasky, who explained his modest figure by saying that he would take a chance on being able to use the beams on another job, but pointing out that he would have to take out special liability insurance to guard him against the possible consequences for one of his helpers—very likely, Mr. Perlasky thought—that the slightest tampering with the house would lead to an instantaneous and tumultuous collapse. His recruitment of a work crew might, he felt, encounter reluctance, but as for himself he had once spent seventy-two hours before being rescued from a Kentucky coal-mine catastrophe and had thereafter felt very little apprehension at anything. If Mr. Blandings wished to take advantage of this price, he had best act swiftly, Mr. Perlasky concluded; if the house were to fall down before he had the chance to remove its parts in order, he could scarcely make so favorable a proposal, and the splintering of the falling beams would sharply decrease his salvage values.

It was at this point that Mr. Blandings' stout heart failed him. He put Mr. Perlasky off with paltering evasions, but when he faced Mrs. Blandings with the news he had no alternative but to be brave. The entire Blandings restoration project must be put off to another, happier time. They had their land; they could now afford the luxury of delay while they made their minds up for the next proper step. Whatever they were eventually to do with or to the old house, Mr. Blandings had no wish to begin it until prices were "right"; currently, every trend curve in Wall Street counseled caution and postponement.

• • •

The forces that were to make prices "right" in the residential construction industry were not known to Mr. Blandings, but he did not know that he did not know them. He was sure, however, that the following spring would be the time to resume constructive thoughts. The summer had vanished anyway, in the course of the dealings with Mr. Funkhauser, Mr. Apollonio, and Mr. Perlasky, and an early autumn had set in. The children were home from camp and back in school; by the strange alchemy of childhood, they were now full of gleeful excitement about a house in the country—the more utterly colonial, the better. Some camp counselor on whom they had a crush must have said some accidental kind word about the eighteenth century, the Blandings surmised. They were happy, but their children's new eagerness would not hurry them. Probably the worst and most frequent mistake of home builders, Mr. and Mrs. Blandings agreed, was trying to rush things; when you were planning the house that was to be your home all the rest of your life few courses were as rash as rushing pell-mell into things without the benefit of decisions that were ripened and matured. What was the delay of one season compared to the everlasting satisfactions of having planned deeply and planned well?

It was heartening, this degree of understanding

between husband and wife. Mr. and Mrs. Blandings let the gray winter close in on them with an almost Oriental calm.

The calm was broken one February evening when Mr. Blandings engaged in calculations. Looking to the spring, he was figuring up his expenses to date. The first footing of the figures left him dissatisfied; he did the whole thing again, and the results were the same. Then it was that Mr. Blandings came face to face with the inexorable fact that in land cost, brokerage, survey expenses, legal exactions, Mr. Apollonio's fee, Mr. Funkhauser's blueprints, Mr. Perlasky's estimate, and a round dozen of other items all small in themselves, but none of them foreseen in the beginning, he had so far spent or all but spent a total of $13,381.34—and the rasp of one saw or the blow of one hammer was yet to be heard on Bald Mountain.

"Don't be surprised when the children grow up to be guttersnipes, hearing words like that in their own living room," said Mrs. Blandings.

V

Second Lamp of Architecture

"We can fix up that old house," said Mr. Simms, looking at it with affection. "Of course we can. You can fix up *any* structure that's still standing. The sills and the chimney certainly couldn't be worse, I grant you, but I'm amazed at how solid the beams are."

Good, the Blandings inwardly exulted. They would "restore" their house after all, just as God had meant them to when first He brought them to it. Mr. Simms was saying they could.

Mr. Simms was the new architect. The Blandings loved him, and were full of repinings that they had not found him in the first place. After searching the Eastern seaboard for a successor to Mr. Funkhauser, they had discovered Mr. Simms living not five miles away from Bald Mountain in the next town to the north—a distinguished member of his profession, deferred to by men with names more publicized than his own, author of two books on the early history of his state's architecture, alert, vital, and humorous: the obvious answer to home builders in trouble. *Why,* thought Mrs. Blandings, in vexation, *why* had it been Mr. Funkhauser that her husband had met at that ill-fated cocktail party when it might so easily, and so infinitely better, have been Mr. Simms? There was a whole world of difference between this distinguished native of their own adopted countryside and an overeducated Brooklyn boy trying to create a phony château out of an old drover's home. The Blandings had known Mr. Simms for a week, and they hung on his words. He was It. The plans for the future, obscure through the long winter, were clear again with the coming of the Blandings' second spring.

"On the other hand," Mr. Simms continued, "fixing up any house as neglected as this one is going to cost a lot of money. Just about as much money as building a new house of the same size, I'd say, and I question whether you'd have what you want when you get through. My advice is to start afresh."

Very well, said the Blandings inwardly, we'll start afresh. Now that they thought about it again, starting afresh was really what they wanted most in all the world to do. Nothing so healthy as acknowledging an error and wiping the slate clean.

"And yet I'm very fond of that old house," said Mr. Simms. "I've known it for years, and it's made me sick to see it slowly going to ruin. It hasn't any fanlight window like the old Bennett house down the road, and there's no beauty of detail anywhere; after all, it's been a working farmhouse from the day it was built to the day old Hackett's father died; but, by George, I just don't know of any house around here that's more foursquare and honest than this one.

"I don't mean foursquare *literally,*" he said with a light laugh. "I guess you'd have to jack up that west corner at least three feet to make the floors level again. Too bad you didn't happen to buy it ten years ago. We could have fixed it up in jig time, then."

Later that morning Mr. Simms showed the Blandings a portfolio of houses he had designed, all of them within a twenty-mile radius of Bald Mountain, and the last lingering uncertainties in Mr. Blandings' mind about homes and home building disappeared completely. The houses were superb. They clung low to the ground, their long horizontal lines were infinitely restful; they breathed ease, peace, security, charm, taste, quiet, and serenity. And comfort; oh, what comfort. Mr. Simms's houses used all the resources of modernity; they had not a trace of obsequiousness to the Past. But neither were they cheesebox modern; they were good without reference to Age or Period, proudly and quietly in their own right. Even a stair rail or a porch rail, as Mr. Simms designed it, was lovely to look at; an utterly simple rectangle in cross section, but with a faint camber at the top to make it gratify the eye and hand. Mr. Simms was a cause for rejoicing.

• • •

Mr. and Mrs. Blandings had begun their home-building career with the assumption that they had $20,000 to spend. When the real-estate man had pointed out to them that $10,000 for land and $10,000 for "restoration" came to this precise figure, the logic and the arithmetic had seemed simple indeed. It was somewhat more clouded now, but not hopelessly so, not hopelessly so by a long shot, Mr. Blandings reassured himself. Manifestly, with some $13,000 invested so far, you couldn't skimp on the building by putting up a mere $7000 bungalow. That would be stupid—although Mr. Simms had built some charming examples for that figure or less, and was the open advocate of smallness, modesty, and prudence. They were models of good taste and deft arrangement, but they didn't provide, said Mr. Blandings, hunting for just the right expression, room enough to swing a cat in. No; the house the Blandings would have to build (as they slowly and unconsciously abandoned all last thoughts of restoring the old house) would have to cost that same $10,000 they had had in mind since the beginning. Prices were somewhat higher now—the winter had seen a general increase in index figures—so an adjusted figure would probably stand something closer to $12,500. That was the figure to shoot at, anyway. It might come out a little on the high side, but you couldn't spend all your life worrying about $500 here or there. When the Blandings' children grew up, they certainly wouldn't thank their parents for having built a house in which they couldn't entertain their young friends with room and to spare. Here was another summer coming when they would have to go to camp again—all for the lack of a true home for the family as a whole.

What the Blandings wanted, they explained to Mr. Simms, was simple enough: a two-story house in quiet, modern, good taste; frame and brick-veneer construction; something to blend with the older architectural examples that dotted the countryside around them, but no slavish imitation of times past. It would be, in effect, a bringing up to date of the Old House, with obvious modifications dictated by the difference between the eighteenth and twentieth centuries and by the difference between the profession of farming, for which the Old House had been constructed, and advertising, which should somehow be exemplified in the New.

"Excellent," said Mr. Simms; "you people really understand your problem."

On the first floor the Blandings wanted a good-sized living room with a fireplace; a dining room, pantry, and kitchen; a small lavatory. On the second, there would be four bedrooms and accompanying baths: one for Mr. and Mrs. Blandings; one for guests; one each for the growing girls. There must be a roomy cellar for goings-on, vague but essential, beyond mere plumbing and heating; a good attic for storage; plenty of closets and a couple of nice porches. "We're certainly asking for the minimum," said Mr. Blandings.

Mr. Simms said that if they really meant it, they could have this for very close to their figure, if they'd cut out two of the bathrooms, which ran into money in a dozen different ways, many of them remote from the eye, like the size of the hot-water heater in the cellar, or the septic tank in the flower-strewn fields. Mrs. Blandings said she was sorry, but two bathrooms would not do. That might as well be clear at the outset. Mr. Simms agreed that Mrs. Blandings had not left it ambiguous.

A series of lovely days began. For the swiftly approaching summertime, the Blandings rented a pleasant little cottage not far away from the foot of their mountain; Mrs. Blandings would stay there until the autumn, the children would stay until camp time, while Mr. Blandings came up for week ends and his August vacation. Mr. Simms ("How *well* he wears," exulted Mrs. Blandings after a fortnight) developed a habit that the Blandings found delightful; almost every Saturday and Sunday afternoon he would arrive at the Blandings' cottage, bringing, at some bother to himself, a drawing board, T square, and triangles.

"We might as well do this whole thing together," he said. "I've got to design it, but you've got to live in it. We'll collaborate."

So in the sweet, warm afternoons, Mr. Simms and the Blandings would confer and plan together, and Mr. Simms would draw the scrupulously neat, light lines of his first tentative plans. The Blandings were being lucky at last, and they reveled in the total reversal of their fortunes. Their architect had flawless good taste, yet he was not rigid in his own ideas; if Mrs. Blandings (as frequently) or Mr. Blandings (as more rarely) had a good idea, Mr. Simms would snap it up eagerly, and no one would ever guess, from his simple enthusiasms for an amateur's ideas, that he was one of the gold-medalists of his profession.

Things went swimmingly. The Blandings girls saw in Mr. Simms a marked resemblance to Charles Boyer, except for accent, and mooned after him endlessly. Betsy, freed of her dental bands, was now able to pursue soulfulness and went so far as to plead for remission from camp, so that she might act as Mr. Simms's assistant. In the midst of the new happiness, Mr. Blandings had only one complaint. "Simms makes everything too small," he said. "I think his ideas are wonderful, but, my God, if there's one thing I don't want in the country, it's to feel *cramped.*"

To this criticism Mr. Simms replied that he was watching the cubage. The Blandings had never

In the sweet, warm afternoons, Mr. Simms and the Blandings would confer and plan together.

heard of cubage before, but Mr. Simms explained that there was nothing recondite about it; it was merely the overall cubic content that roof and walls enclosed. A rough rule of thumb was that, for the sort of house the Blandings obviously wanted, with quality materials and tasteful finish, the cost would be about forty-five to fifty cents a cubic foot. This sounded dirt cheap to Mr. and Mrs. Blandings; there was nothing in their past lives to make them conscious of the traps that algebra held for the unwary in an exponential equation of no higher than the third power. Mr. Simms, they felt (and told him), was holding a little too tight a rein on the cubage, good fault that it was.

Mr. Simms sighed a little. "Look," he said. "You ought to be fully aware that this $15,000 more or less"—(Mr. Blandings winced inwardly)—"this $15,000 more or less that you're calling the cost of your house doesn't get you moved into it with light bulbs in all the sockets and a pack of cigarettes on every table. It's for the *shell* of the house—well, not the shell exactly, because it does include the plumbing equipment, and your heater, and so on, but it doesn't figure a stove or a refrigerator or a washing machine, and other things like that. And you've got a water supply to think of."

("Good God, the water supply," said Mr. Blandings in the silences of his brain. He had mentally turned on all the glittering chromium faucets in the bathrooms a hundred times and they had gushed forth like Moses' rock, but he had somehow not traced their bounteous supply back to its source. Not that he had forgotten about it; he just hadn't had much time to think about it. . . .)

"I just don't want you to wake up some morning in a state of shock, that's all," he heard Mr. Simms conclude. "If you were to ask me right now, I'd guess that what we have on the drawing board here looks more like an $18,000 house than a $15,000 one."

"Maybe we'd better cut out *one* bathroom," said Mr. Blandings, pleased with himself now that he had the water-supply problem well in hand.

"I will not hazard the children's health in a house with three bathrooms," said Mrs. Blandings. She looked so flushed with annoyance that Mr. Simms clamped his jaw shut on a decorously jocose remark that had just occurred to him about privies. There was a time for everything, but this was not it.

"Where," asked Mr. Blandings, one week end later, "are we going to *put* the house?"

It was a simple question, fraught with peril. It made suddenly and gapingly apparent a basic flaw in understanding between client and architect. Mr. Simms had assumed that the three criteria for the site were level ground, a good view, and nearness to the road. He was too experienced an architect to make such an assumption without putting it into words, but somehow he had, and now there was hell to pay. For several days before this crisis arose, Mr. Blandings and Mrs. Blandings had been notably aloof from one another; they had obviously been having bad fourth-bathroom trouble and had spoken to one another in Mr. Simms's presence with cold infrequence. Suddenly, they had common cause: man and his mate against the hated stranger at the cave's mouth. What they had assumed all along, they said fiercely to Mr. Simms, was that the new house would burrow into the side of a hill just as the old house did. They saw no reason why this should alarm, discommode, or depress the architect in any way. It came to them only slowly, and with much feverish impromptu sketching by Mr. Simms, that if their house was to jut into a hillside, all the windows on its north side would be considerably below grade, and that this situation could not be cured merely by substituting solid wall for window openings. Eventually the Blandings altered their concept of the site and the relation of ground slopes to architectural plans and elevations, but more because the snow-shoveling problem of a long driveway occurred to Mr. Blandings than because they saw the force of Mr. Simms's real objections. The crisis abated, but Mr. Simms needed occasional heavy drafts of self-control over the next month when Mrs. Blandings would now and again refer to "Mr. Simms's mistake" in placing a handsome set of casement windows beneath the grass.

So, without too much unhappiness, the house was again planned to lie on the spot for which Mr. Simms had begun to design it. Thereupon another problem swiftly arose in the Blandings' minds. The new house was too close to the old house—the two buildings would clash impossibly.

"I certainly hate to see you tear that old house down," said Mr. Simms. "But I guess you've got to face it that you've either got to tear it down or fix it up." In five quick minutes he drew a little sketch of what you could do with the old house, so neat, charming, and ingenious that Mr. Blandings wondered for a moment why Mr. Simms had not proposed doing that in the first place, instead of building any new house at all. Could he, dare he, make such a comment now? He thought of Mrs. Blandings, and what a demure girl she had been, her first year out of Bryn Mawr, and decided that in prudence he had better carry his question with him unspoken to the grave.

"I guess," said Mr. Blandings instead, "we'll tear it down. We'll tear it down right here and now before what I once heard described as its 'genuine antique value' costs me any more money to get rid of." There came back to him with a momentary bitterness the year-old letter from the real-estate man in which that phrase occurred. It made him think how happy he had been in the days when he had been a plain city dweller, and Van Cortlandt Park had been away uptown, and he had never seen the Old Hackett Property. His underlip suddenly quivered, like a mistreated servant girl's. Shortly, he put on a stolid mask and sought a new interview with Mr. Perlasky, and learned that the price of removing the house would now be $1075—labor had gone up, and what was more,

Mr. Perlasky no longer knew for certain of a job on which he could use the old beams.

Mr. Perlasky came to work a week later with two assistants, and within an hour the ground around the old house was strewn with ravished shingles. The old chimney, with its delicate projecting course of stone at the top, was wrecked into the fragments of the raw gneiss that someone had quarried with such pain so long ago, and the rock-hard clay that had molded solidly into the chinks between it. Mr. Blandings could not bear to look as the lovely old building, still untouched at the bottom except by the cold hands of the years, became raggeder and raggeder at its second story, as if a slow, deadly acid were consuming it.

There came a day when nothing but the frame remained, enclosing the stump of the chimney and the massive fireplaces around which Mr. and Mrs. Blandings had once planned to sit and rock and mull the wine and patch the quilts and roast the apples as, with graceful serenity, they entered the twilight of their lives.

"Watch it!" cried Mr. Perlasky, as a final load of filth flung itself out of the sky and landed at Mr. Blandings' country brogues. He glared at the blue vault of the heavens and then at the pile at his feet. "My equity," he said softly to himself. "My $8400; there it lies. Why didn't I light cigars with it? Why didn't I spend it on liquor, narcotics, whores, and the subornation of perjury? I could have had quite a time for myself on $8400—and the day of disillusion would have been no more bitter than this."

As Mr. Blandings watched Mr. Perlasky and his men struggling to unship the beams, he came to wonder whether he had done *anything* since the day he first saw the Old Hackett Property except follow one demented decision with another. The error of buying the house was not corrected by the error of tearing it down. For a structure that had so affrighted Mr. Apollonio, the old Hackett house was giving up now only with the most hideous convulsions; the doweled and mortised beams were clasped together like two lovers in a single grave whom not even death could part. When Mr. Perlasky showed up the following day with only one helper and explained that the other one had ruptured himself in the final effort that had torn the framing loose, Mr. Blandings' sympathies were not for the sufferer with the protruding intestines but totally and exclusively for himself. The Hackett house was down; he had obliterated a relic of history at a cost to himself of $8400 for the house, $50 for the advice to take it down, and $1075 for following the advice. The total was $9525, and what Mr. Blandings was sure were the beginnings of an obscure ailment in his duodenum.

The evening came when the last truckload of undifferentiated rubbish rattled away down the mountain, and only an empty, trodden, stone-girt rectangle of earth remained to show where a living house had been. The great lilac tree stood alone, now, its companion of the years banished from its side. Mr. Blandings remembered another evening, a year ago, when the first tiny, tentative question about the worth and fitness of the old house had first been raised. He remembered who had raised it. He wanted very much to ask Mrs. Blandings if *she* remembered, and if she was pleased, now, with the finale to which it had led. As he was about to clear his throat, he heard his wife sigh.

"I *hope* you were wise in taking down the old house," said Mrs. Blandings.

VI
Happy Interlude

The vigorous young brook that went dodging down the rocks behind the Blandings' building site had always been referred to, during real-estate negotiations, as "the trout stream"; even Mr. Simms called it that, now. Mr. Blandings did not see how so narrow and restless a watercourse could give even a very small trout the needed room for backing and parking, but he didn't care, for even in his darker moments he loved to watch its gaiety and listen to its endless song. In a more practical mood, it came to him that the brook would be his source of water supply. Mr. Simms had looked dubious at this proposal, but had said only, "I think it dries up in August." When Mr. Blandings imprisoned some of the crystal waters in a five-gallon carboy, he was disappointed at their brown turbidity, and was not happy to see graceful, swirling fragments of something or other settle slowly to the bottom.

For $6.50 the near-by Stoop Biological Laboratories rendered an analysis of the contents, warning him that the waters were unpotable; it suggested the presence of cows in an upper field as the reason behind the intense activity visible even at the lowest power of microscope magnification.

The biological laboratory warned Mr. Blandings that the waters were unpotable; it suggested the presence of cows.

Mr. Blandings had often seen the cows, he now came to realize; they belonged to a neighborhood farmer from whom he had expected to buy milk when his days of residency began. He had thought happily about the cows, but as a source of nourishment, not of *B. coli*, and it had certainly never occurred to him that their eupeptically flawless elimination might interfere with his plans for his house. As things were turning out, the laboratory said, he had better drill a well.

Mr. Blandings sighed, but bowed to what must be. An artesian well, which Mr. Simms told him he must have, sounded expensive, but it also sounded exciting. The word "artesian" had always suggested to Mr. Blandings a spurting forth from the earth of waters possessing some marked therapeutic or purgative quality. Now he learned that in common usage an artesian well was merely a well drilled deep into rock, as opposed to a well dug into thirty or forty feet of earth to catch the surface waters. Even in his boyhood, Mr. Blandings remembered, a shallow well and a hand pump had sufficed all but the wealthiest; ladies of the most fragile quality in those days drank with impunity from wells and streams whose waters would fell a stevedore today. The race was certainly getting brittle, Mr. Blandings reflected, when a man dared not drink from his own sylvan brook—but still, the cold sparkling waters from a rock would be something to savor. Mr. Simms offered the name of a well driller in the adjoining county who would drill Mr. Blandings a well at $4.50 a foot for the first three hundred feet, and $6 a foot thereafter, if necessary. When a fortnight later one Mr. John Tesander, well driller, appeared on the Blandings' acres with a bright-red drill rig that looked like a foreshortened hook-and-ladder fire truck, a new richness came into Mr. Blandings' life with him.

• • •

Mr. Tesander, who spoke English heavily tinctured by birth and upbringing in the mountains of Bosnia, was one of those skilled workmen who restored a man's faith in his kind. He wore gold-rimmed glasses and had a scholar's face, but his forearms, biceps, and chest were sculptured by a quarter of a century of heavy, cheerful toil. Mr. Blandings was momentarily dismayed by the empiricism of selecting a well site ("I sinks she might as good go here as anywheres," Mr. Tesander had said, indicating a wide area seeming no different from any other half acre on Bald Mountain), but once Mr. Tesander settled down to work, his doubts disappeared. That Mr. Tesander had the skill of a surgeon and the equanimity of a lama was quickly apparent. As Mr. Blandings watched him maneuver his rig to the selected spot and begin to unload his gear, he felt new hope and cheer surge through him, not merely for the success of the well but for the whole great Blandings Project. There was something about Mr. Tesander's quiet, tolerant good nature that Mr. Blandings found infinitely soothing. The job would probably keep him on the site between five and seven weeks, Mr. Tesander said; Mr. Blandings resolved that he himself would spend every possible day between now and the completion of the well watching this quiet aristocrat of heavy labor at his craft. Mr.

Blandings' summer vacation from Banton & Dascomb and the Knapp laxative account was due to begin in another fortnight, and then he would do nothing whatever but don a pair of overalls (he was learning to call them "overhalls" as local dialect insisted) and sit on a grassy bank and watch Mr. Tesander and learn how to drill a well. His soul needed it.

When Mr. Blandings hurried back to Bald Mountain after a perfunctory summer work week in the city, he found Mr. Tesander and his helper literally poised to begin the major job. They had dug a hole, six feet by six, as far as they could go with shovels; they had jacked the drill rig up on its axles, to level and secure it. A miniature blacksmith shop—anvil, sledge, bellows, coke pile, water quench—was set up neatly under a spreading oak. As Mr. Blandings watched, Mr. Tesander and a helper unshipped the long, glistening 500-pound drill bit that was to sink the well. Into the mandrel at its head they looped and rove the end of a 500-foot cable of twisted steel strands; it went up and over a pulley in the tower of the rig, then down and under a pulley in the walking beam, and thence was guided back to a drum from which it could be paid out as the drill demanded a longer and longer halter on its dark, downward passage.

Mr. Tesander checked everything over one last time, and steadied the huge free-swinging pendulum of drill and cable over the exact spot where water was someday expected to flow. His helper cranked the rig's heavy motor, and the moment had arrived. The motor roared; the rig shook with an ague; and Mr. Tesander cautiously let in a clutch. The drill bit rose, hung poised for an instant, then plunged to the end of its stroke and dealt the earth a staggering blow. Mr. Blandings' well was being drilled! At last, some instrument was at work more dramatic than a draftsman's pencil, and there would be something to show, pretty soon, for the passage of fifteen months, and for the tears and struggles that had so far been the lot of the Blandings on Bald Mountain.

Mr. Blandings spent every available hour watching his well in process. The drill bit had now sunk out of sight so that Mr. Blandings could create, at pleasure, the illusion that it was already a hundred feet down; how wonderful it would be, he thought, if his well should suddenly blow in with a gusher of water that spouted to the top of the near-by oak. And hadn't people drilled for water and struck oil? He confided his fantasies to Mr. Tesander, who treated them kindly but warned against overoptimism. Both these things had happened in the long history of well drilling, but infrequently, and, of record, never at twelve feet down.

The rig's motor roared and stank; the walking beam rose and fell, and rose and fell, lifting the bit three feet each time, letting it down with a shattering slam and instantly repeating its cycle—at a beat, Mr. Blandings estimated, of some thirty-five strokes to the minute when all was going smoothly. Mr. Tesander, his right hand encased in an enormous glove, would damp the whipping vibrations of the cable as it went from taut to slack every time the bit struck bottom. "No yob for man wiz rheumatism," he bellowed happily at Mr. Blandings over the general roar.

No, thought Mr. Blandings, and no yob for man wiz anxiety neurosis, either. Any one of a dozen emergencies could flash into being any instant the rig was working: the worst, which was also the most likely, was that the drill would catch and jam on the rocky circumference of its close-fitting hole; if it did, the rig would wrench itself silly on its next attempted upstroke, even before the motor could stall. Mr. Tesander recounted for Mr. Blandings the various jobs during the last twenty years on which this or some allied misfortune had befallen him. Once he had gone down and down to a total of 850 feet and never encountered a drop of water all the way. Mr. Blandings' mouth went dry at the thought. The client, Mr. Tesander explained, had been a wealthy and eccentric old tyrant who wanted his well just there and nowhere else; he would permit no second hole anywhere on his 300 acres. At the 851st foot the cable had snapped. "Dann, I loss' my schtring," said Mr. Tesander. ("String," Mr. Blandings discovered, was short for "string of tools," which described the bit, stem, and mandrel of the drill, plus whatever in the way of drill jars might be necessary on a tough job.) "I go fishing for it, but I never catch my schtring again. Old man died same week. Cost me t'ousand dollar. Some yobs I make money, some I lose my shirt. I never can tell." He smiled happily at the memory of past ill-fortunes and the hazards of his occupation, and carefully loosed a clutch to pay out another two inches of cable to the drill bit.

Father of us all, thought Mr. Blandings, from what deep wells of Your devising does this man draw his beautiful calm, his total equanimity? I pay him $4.50 for every foot he sinks this shaft for me, and he doesn't know whether he's going to make a hundred dollars or so with all his sweaty, vein-bursting labor, or whether he's going to lose his "string" and his shirt with it. And it doesn't seem to bother him. He was put into the world to drill wells, so he drills 'em, and so far as I can see that's all that counts with him. Why can't everyone be like him? Why can't *I* be like him?

Mr. Tesander declutched his walking beam, throttled his motor down to a splutter, and threw another lever; the big cable drum revolved for a long minute and then the drill bit came up out of the earth, twisting and glinting in the sunlight. Then Mr. Blandings began to see the purpose of the blacksmith's apparatus: the neatly glowing coke fire, the ready anvil, and the sledge. While his helper offered an occasional Delsarte gesture, Mr. Tesander flung a heavy guard plank over the hole the drill had made, and applied two giant wrenches to the bit. After four inches of oily, gleaming screw threads had exposed themselves, the bit came free; Mr. Tesander struggled it into the fire and applied a new one to his string of tools. By the time he had his rig working again, the bit in the fire was a cherry red. With languidly incompetent assistance from his helper, he plopped it on the anvil, and taking up the sledge (which Mr. Blandings had found awkward to lift at all), began to rain a fury of blows upon its glowing conical tip. Even above the noise of the rig, they rang with the pitch and frequency of a fire gong, and Mr. Blandings could see them reshaping the dulled tip into the chisel faces that would cut loose still more of the dense, variegated barriers that stood between him and a water supply. Mr. Tesander brushed off the scale with a glove that smoked when he touched the red steel, and a moment later heaved the whole bit, gently but urgently, into the caldron of water that stood at his right. There was a furious boil and hiss that lasted almost a minute, and when it was over Mr. Tesander pulled an old envelope out of his pants pocket, from it stuffed a corncob pipe, and slowly sat down on the bank beside Mr. Blandings, puffing tobacco smoke in perfect comfort. “Warm day,” said Mr. Tesander.

It was, Mr. Blandings agreed; he looked at Mr. Tesander’s well-browned skin as it showed through his ripped and tattered undershirt, and saw, with a vast feeling of inferiority, that it was as dry as a granite statue. Well, he thought, someday *he* would be able to work like that in a warm sun and not sweat; someday after he was a seasoned country dweller and could fell an old oak in an afternoon, raining a precision of ax blows on its trunk with a virtuosity like Mr. Tesander’s with the sledge.

The word “oak” made him think of beams, which made him think of the old Hackett house, which made him think of Mr. Perlasky, which made him think of $9525. Sitting quietly beside Mr. Tesander, he burst into perspiration.

VII

History Is as History Does

There is the most *hideous* thing going on not half a mile from where our property ends," said Mrs. Blandings when her husband came home from a satisfying vacation afternoon watching Mr. Tesander at the well. "Right on the *road!*"

The way she spoke suggested in Mr. Blandings' mind the spectacle of a boa constrictor publicly squeezing the life out of a goat in the middle of the byway that led down Bald Mountain into Lansdale Town. Mr. Blandings said nothing but paused on the verge of pouring the vermouth into the gin, and looked up with his eyebrows cocked at the angle of impatience that meant, Well, go on.

Mrs. Blandings gathered herself slowly for the revelation. "Honestly!" she said, "I'm just *sick* about it, literally *sick*. You just haven't any *idea.*"

Mr. Blandings resumed activity and splashed enough liquid from a bottle that said VERMOUTH, FRENCH TYPE, MADE IN GALION, OHIO to color the gin a perceptible amber.

"If it keeps up, it will be the end of *everything,*" said Mrs. Blandings.

Mr. Blandings added the ice and stirred. His wife faced him in obvious emotion.

"Somebody is building a *house!*" she burst forth.

Mr. Blandings set down the untasted Martini with a crash. "What!" he cried. "Where? Who?"

"I've been telling you," said Mrs. Blandings, quivering. "Right down by before you turn off for the Grovers'. A horrid, nasty little house with two rooms and a porch *right on the road!*"

Mr. Blandings dismissed all thought to make light of things. This was a crisis: the principle of Protection was involved. "Even with thirty-one and a half acres you've still got plenty of Protection," the real-estate man had said, consolingly, at the time of the last area shrinkage. Was even this, now, to prove a false assurance?

"Can you *see* it?" Mr. Blandings demanded.

"*See* it?" said Mrs. Blandings. "Of course you can *see* it. I've told you three times, it's *right on the road!*"

"I mean can you see it from *Our Place?*" he snapped. He was tense; this was the crucial point of the inquiry.

"I don't know," said Mrs. Blandings with a blurred moan. "But I'm as positive as I'm sitting here that you can see it in the *winter.* When the leaves are all off the trees, I just know that *at least the top of it* is going to be in *plain sight.*"

This was just about as bad as anything could be. Scarcely over a year after the Blandings had bought the top of a virgin mountain, Blight had appeared—Blight that could almost be seen when the transient, masking leaves were no longer there to hide it. In New York, the Blandings' dignified seventeen-story-and-penthouse apartment building stood next door to a garage; four doors farther up the block was a "converted" brownstone on whose top floor a drunken maniac had methodically slain a family of five one Thanksgiving Day just two years ago. It was a quiet, orderly block with a liquor store on one corner and a funeral home on another; rather a higher-class block than the average on New York's fashionable upper East Side. The Blandings found little in it to complain about except perhaps the window display of the abdominal-truss manufacturer's showroom next to the garage. But now, in the country hills, their idyl of peace and solitude was being shattered by the building of a house not 2640 feet from the southeast corner that marked the end of their own, their private land. It was the last straw.

"It's a horrid, beastly little *bungalow,*" said Mrs. Blandings, "and it's going to have a tar-paper roof and they're going to paint it a bright *green.* That Hackett creature sold him two acres for it."

"Who's *he?* Where did you pick all this up?" asked Mr. Blandings.

"In the drugstore," said Mrs. Blandings. "It couldn't be worse. The man is a *stonemason,* and they have *ten* children, and *she* keeps goats. I could simply *weep.* If we're going to have a *shanty* right in our *back yard,* I guess we might just as well give up the whole *thing.*"

Even when buoyed up by the contents of a second shakerful of still paler Martinis, Mr. Blandings could not help taking a drastic view of the invasion of Bald Mountain. There was no question that Protection was a mockery; no question that Mr. Hackett had done one more traitorous, treacherous thing to Mr. and Mrs. Blandings; selling a miserable two-acre wedge of his mountain to a *stonemason* with *children* and *goats,* on which the stonemason was now busily erecting, with his own hands, what was nothing more or less than a *bungalow* that would be painted *green*. "What a nasty, mean-spirited thing to do," said Mrs. Blandings. "And stupid, too. He sold those two acres for a total of $65. It's just impossible to figure these country people out."

Next day, as they drove toward Lansdale Town, Mr. and Mrs. Blandings stopped off to study the whole situation at length. An industrious young man in the gray costume of a stonemason was indeed at work, nailing a narrow tongue-and-groove siding to the framing of a structure that could not have been much more than fifteen feet square. "Howdy," he said, as the Blandings stopped, ostensibly out of a neighborly intention of passing the time of day. "Thought I'd put me up a little shack where we could bring our two kids summers. Gets pretty hot right in the middle of the village, and this Bald Mountain is just about the finest country in the whole state, you ask me. You folks live up this way?"

Shack, thought Mrs. Blandings; that's certainly the word for it. She was relieved a trifle that the ten children of her overheard conversation were reduced to a more manageable quantity. But only a trifle. First thing that morning she and her husband had climbed to the highest corner of their acres with a pair of binoculars and anxiously swept the countryside to see if they could discover evidence of the abode that was to be the ruination of their view, their peace of mind, their solitude. The binoculars' two circular fields of view had a tendency to twitch and decline to fuse in Mr. Blandings' hands, but Mrs. Blandings held the glasses before her as steadily as a mariner and was sure she could detect a small triangle with a white gleam which could well be one of the eaves of the stonemason's dwelling.

"Yes," said Mrs. Blandings. "We live farther up the road."

"I don't recognize you," said the young man. "I was born right down in the town here and I know every face within fifteen miles. I guess you must be city people decided to get wise to yourself."

This is ridiculous, Mrs. Blandings thought. He's treating us like intruders.

"That's right," said Mr. Blandings with a

sudden, synthetic country heartiness. "Our name is Blandings and we've bought the old Hackett place at the top of the mountain."

"Well, for God's sake," said the young man. "Speak of the devil! I was reading a piece about you folks in the newspaper just last night and I said to my wife, some of the damnedest things can happen around this part of the country, those were my very words."

The Blandings exchanged lightning glances. They were subscribers to the Lansdale *Blade* and their weekly copy had arrived yesterday afternoon, to lie unopened on the living-room table. Apparently their neglect of it had deprived them of some experience.

"Yes, sir," the young man went on, "some of the damnedest things. You got one consolation, anyway—a lot of people think old Mrs. Prutty is pretty hipped on that sort of business. Got too much time on her hands ever since her husband got run over by the milk truck down to Gatti's Tavern, where he didn't have no business anyway."

There was no faintest clue in any of this for the uneasy Blandings. They dared not exchange another glance, but each knew the other shared a deep alarm. They also knew they were becoming very uncomfortable in the young man's presence; they had come to observe and assess him, and perhaps to grant him, grudgingly if at all, the privilege of being their neighbor. But now it was he who had them on the defensive—about what they did not know and felt small heart to inquire. Mr. Blandings attempted an ambiguous set of jocularities which might seem later to hold some universal application, and sought to signify the end of the visit by putting his car in gear.

"I wouldn't take it too hard if I was you," said the young man. "It's just one of them nine-day tempests in a teapot. Give 'em time and they'll forget it. Too bad it had to happen, but don't let it get you down."

The Blandings exchanged worried speculations as they drove on down to Lansdale Town for the Saturday shopping. It was not pleasant to be the subject of newspaper notoriety, particularly when you were the conspicuous stranger, known to those you did not know yourself. It was even less pleasant to know that there were allegations about you, obviously unfavorable, but not to know what they were. In the village, Mr. Blandings was certain that people were looking at him in a funny way, although the occasional how-de-do's of the shopping tour seemed friendly enough. He went into Scadron's stationery store to buy a New York paper, and furtively eyed a mound of Lansdale *Blades*. They were stacked with the print upside down, to discourage browsing, but at least Mr. Blandings could see that they carried no eight-column headline with his name in it. He would have to wait until he got back to the cottage to find out what this was all about. Meanwhile, he could feel an air of furtiveness enshrouding him; while Mrs. Blandings pursued an endless conversation with the butcher he tried to while away a moment at the soda fountain next door, but his request for a Coca-Cola was as hoarse and tremulous as if he were asking for absinthe before his breakfast.

Back in the seclusion of the Blandings' summer cottage, he could, at first, find nothing in the Lansdale *Blade.* All the headlines seemed dull; a few were incomprehensible. Mr. Blandings scrutinized page one for the third time. He came again on

HISTORICAL SOCIETY
BLASTS "VANDALISM"

but that this could in any way apply to him never crossed his mind until beneath it, he suddenly saw

Censure Vote Passed Re
Destruction of Famed Bald Mountain Edifice

"Oh, my God," groaned Mr. Blandings, and in fascinated horror read on:

> The usually sedate semimonthly meeting of the good ladies of the Lansdale Historical Society was turned into a scene of uproar at

last Tuesday's gathering on the second floor of the Public Library building when Mrs. Bildad Prutty reported to those present the total demolition by its recent New York buyer of the historic old home of the Hackett family situated atop Bald Mountain and commanding one of the most spectacular views in the township since some years before the town itself was founded. Reputed to be the third-oldest house of its kind in the county, and with innumerable historical associations not only for old Lansdale inhabitants but for their fathers and grandfathers before them, the old Hackett house was swiftly demolished and sold by the new owner for a junk value reported to be $1075, according to Mrs. Prutty. The aroused ladies quickly passed a resolution that Mrs. Prutty head a committee to visit the New Yorker responsible and express the official disapproval of the Society at city people buying old houses of literally priceless antique value and then tearing them down like old sheds to make way for tennis courts and swimming pools and fancy new houses better adapted to Long Island and Newport than to this part of the countryside. For the benefit of some of the newer members of the Society, Mrs. Prutty reminded her audience that several years ago the Society raised the sum of $1900 by popular

Mrs. Prutty was authorized to express the official disapproval of the Historical Society.

subscription for the purchase of the old Hackett house and surrounding property to restore it to the original condition it had been in at the time General Gates was reported to have stopped there for several hours to water his horses on the way to the Battle of

Saratoga, over in York state. The deal fell through by being short $750 of the sum of $2650 which Ephemus Hackett testified was the smallest reasonable sum he could accept as the executor of his father's estate, the local probate court upholding this contention. Mrs. Prutty also . . .

The sharp stab of the telephone bell came as a merciful severance between Mr. Blandings and Mrs. Prutty's further revelations. That Mr. Hackett had been willing to sell his whole property a couple of years ago to Mrs. Prutty's Amazons for $2650 had given him enough to absorb for that afternoon, all in itself. That these Amazons were on the brink of presenting him with a document of censure for paying over four times that amount, and then . . .

"New York is calling," said the operator. "Go ahead, New York."

"Hey, Jim," said Bill Cole's voice, "did you tear down that old what-do-you-call-it house without telling me?"

"Why do you want to know?" said Mr. Blandings, spacing his words in a splurting sort of way. "Are you calling me to tell me that you've just married old Mrs. Prutty?"

"What did you say?" asked Mr. Blandings' lawyer.

"Has the Historical Society retained you? I'd just like to know," said Mr. Blandings.

"I don't get you," said Bill Cole. "Are you all right? Listen, what I'm calling for is to tell you I've just had a letter from your Mr. Hackett's lawyer."

"Oh," said Mr. Blandings.

"Listen," said Bill Cole, "don't you know you can't tear down a house on which another man holds a mortgage without getting his express written consent? The old boy is serving notice that under the terms of the mortgage the whole balance of the purchase price is now payable on demand, and this is his demand."

"Deposit another thirty-five cents for another three minutes, please," said she operator. There was a sound in the receiver as of the fracture of a large stick of kindling.

Mr. Blandings held the suddenly blank, wordless instrument in his hand for a moment as if it had been a kitten run over by a tractor. Then he put it down in its cradle and strode to the sideboard.

"I make it a point not to criticize your drinking habits, even when I do not approve of them," said Mrs. Blandings, "but when you tip the bottle up and I can hear it gurgle at least three times, I think I am bound to say that it strikes me as not only unwise, but vulgar."

VIII
Plans and Elevations

During the next few days Mr. Blandings spent most of his time wondering if Banton & Dascomb might be persuaded to send him to New Guinea to establish an agency branch, taking over and liquidating all his personal affairs in the United States of America.

This phase soon passed; things became surprisingly better surprisingly soon. Mr. Blandings wondered whether everybody else's life was such a succession of roller-coaster plunges from elation to despair and swoops back to elation, or whether, as his closest friends and office mates insisted, he was a sufferer from severe emotional instability. Anyway, he had not become the community pariah he had prepared himself to be. The next issue of the Lansdale *Blade*, still not mentioning his name, had unexpectedly changed its tack and come to his defense. "Some of our good local ladies," he had read in the lead editorial, "might perhaps reflect if they are not getting a little too high up on their horses. It seems they are all wrought up over the tearing down of the old Hackett house on Bald Mountain, but we will have to be pardoned for saying that this particular landmark was going to racking ruin for a long time before it finally met its fate, and somehow the townsfolk were never able to get together on any plan to do anything about it before it was sold to a purchaser from the city. The ladies should remember that quite a little new retail trade is developing out of some of the money these big-shot newcomers are spending with us and not take an attitude which will discourage progress."

Very sound, Mr. Blandings thought. A little crass, but very sound; some of the tradesfolk must have pointed out this aspect of things to Mr. Whelpus, the *Blade*'s elderly editor. It gave him a wry sense of discomfiture to be called "big shot," even by inference, when his record of managing his own affairs struck him as so totally incompetent—but perhaps he should take himself at the *Blade*'s assessment, not his own. As for Mr. Hackett and the mortgage, Bill Cole had gone through a legal waving of the hands as the result of which Mr. Hackett, through his attorney, agreed to discontinue his allegation that the whole principal sum of the mortgage was due, provided Mr. Blandings immediately paid him $1000 in hand for its reduction. Mr. Blandings had to do some scraping around to come quickly by this sum, but once he did he found it possible to console himself that reducing a mortgage was, after all, a form of saving. He wrote a modest letter to the Lansdale *Blade*, thanking the editor for his utterance, and pointing out that in any event he had paid, not *been* paid, $1075 for the removal of the Hackett landmark. Peace descended again on the exquisite landscape that was Bald Mountain and the sunny community that was Lansdale Town; the bees droned in the warm air and sucked their nectar from a rippling sea of wildflowers. Mrs. Blandings flitted about their summer cottage in a sunbonnet, and Mr. Blandings went back to his study of Mr. Tesander, drilling at the well. His vacation was in mid-career, and he was resolved that nothing else should blemish it.

But much though he loved Mr. Tesander, he was beginning to feel some slight concern. There were even times when he stopped watching and wished he could stop listening too. This latter he could not do: Mr. Tesander was down 107 feet now, and apparently drilling in iron; a concussion would shake the earth every time the drill took its pulverizing bite, and Mr. Blandings could feel it even when he was so far away he could not hear it. On a poor day Mr. Tesander might make four feet; on a good day he might make eighteen, but one circumstance remained always the same: in his methodical progress through the earth's crust, he was encountering everything in an omnipotent God's creation except water. Mr. Blandings' focus of attention began to shift from his friends the

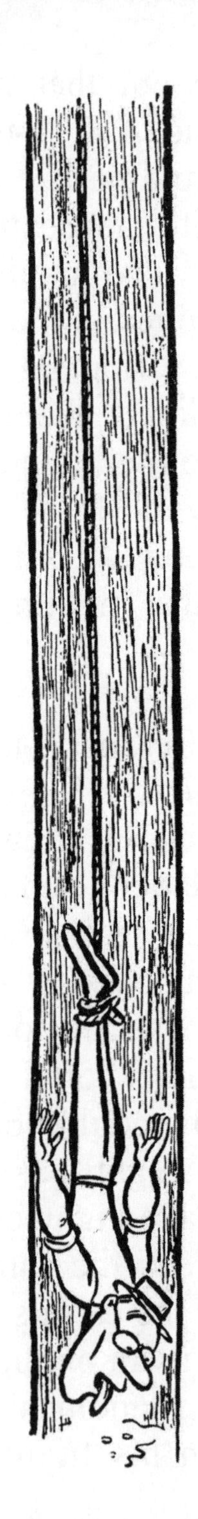

In his methodical progress through the earth's crust, Mr. Tesander was encountering everything in an omnipotent God's creation except water.

Grovers, who had struck a gusher at sixty feet, to the old gentleman that Mr. Tesander had spoken of who had gone down 850 feet and brought forth only dust.

"There ought to be some better way," Mr. Blandings moaned one night after Mr. Tesander had announced that he was down 201 feet in a dry hole and his "string" was stuck. Mrs. Blandings voiced regret that her husband had refused the services of a neighborhood dowser who had offered to pick an infallible well site by means of his forked apple-wood stick, on payment of $25. Mr. Blandings, remembering the specialists' fees paid to Mr. Apollonio and the Stoop Biological Laboratories only for the advice to abandon what he had set himself upon doing, had summarily rejected this proposal and was now wondering if it might not have been worth $25 merely to have Mrs. Blandings on the defensive instead of, as was again the miserable case, vice versa. But his spirits rebounded next day on the news that Mr. Tesander had been able to free his "string" and had also encountered liquids; somewhere in the bowels of geology the drill had struck a fissure through which one-half gallon of water per minute was now flowing into the Blandings' bore. This was far from the twenty gallons per minute which Mr. Blandings had come to think of as a desirable supply, but at least it kept down the cloud of pulverized rock in which Mr. Tesander, unshakable as the Duke of Wellington at his nerve-racking task, had hitherto been working.

A day later, Mr. Tesander struck another water-bearing seam and the flow jumped to four gallons a minute. Mr. Blandings could scarcely have been more transported if it had been petroleum: the thought that he, aided by the invaluable professional skill of Mr. Tesander, had discovered and diverted a secret stream, winding and seeping through the measureless caverns beneath him, gave him a sense of accomplishment and power. What was more, he took delight in discovering the homely methods of wisdom whereby Man, in the person of John Tesander, could know how many gallons of water he was encountering. Left to himself to devise such a measuring system, Mr. Blandings would have been a helpless babe; it fascinated him to discover that all Mr. Tesander needed to make his calculation was an old watch the size of a turkey egg and a small, smooth rock tied to the end of several hundred feet of mason's twine. Mr. Tesander, amused at Mr. Blandings' delight, referred to these objects as "mine shinchronometer und mine hydromometer."

Mr. Blandings insisted, later, on telling his wife every step in the process of measuring the rate of flow of a well. First, Mr. Tesander brought up and unshipped the drill bit, and fastened to his string "the baler"—a tube the same length and diameter as the drill, but hollow and battered. The baler would plunge down the well shaft and strike the subterranean water with a delicious, hollow, echoing splash. Mr. Tesander would haul it up, spurting water, mud, and rock dust from a hundred little punctures, and whack its snout on the earth, whereupon its tongue valve would open and spill silt and water in a luscious, glistening pile.

Eight or ten trips with the baler would clear the well enough for the measuring process to begin. Mr. Tesander would let the stone plummet down the shaft, the twine whirling out on the stick he held in his hands as bearings. When it splashed, Mr. Tesander would pinch the line and mark the length with a deft loop. Then he would haul it part way up and count a long minute on his hammering watch. At the sixtieth second he would find the new, higher splash point, put another loop in his line, and measure the distance between the two. Then he would announce, "Five gallon, now, by God. Going to be a good well!"

"How do you figure it?" asked Mr. Blandings.

"*You* should know; *you* went to school," said Mr. Tesander. The knots were three and a half feet apart, he pointed out: they measured the distance of the water's rise in the minute his watch had ticked off. The bore was six inches in diameter, or half a foot. The volume of a cylinder was *pi* times the square of the diameter times the height, all divided by four. That came out to two thirds of a cubic foot, and, as Mr. Tesander tactfully explained, any fool knew that there were seven and a half gallons to a cubic foot. But you didn't really have to do all that arithmetic, he explained in conclusion; with a six-inch drill, a foot was one and one-half gallons, more or less.

Mr. Blandings was very happy, even though it was apparent that his wife understood no word of his explanation, and cared not a whit. He had five gallons of water at 225 feet, and—excellent sign—the water was rising to within a hundred feet of the surface. Soon, he felt confident, there would be even more. Mr. Blandings had by now irretrievably invested not only dollars but blood on Bald Mountain, but it could no longer be said he had nothing to show. He had water. He would never again see an open fire hydrant splashing on a city street in summer without remembering and appreciating the toil and difficulty with which this precious stuff was wrung from the unwilling rock.

When the bluebells and the columbine faded, the meadow lilies and the wild geranium took up the torch. These in their turn gave way to the black-eyed Susans, the bee balm, and the evening primrose. It would soon be time for the tall, waving asters and the goldenrod. August was well along. "I wish I knew where the time had gone," sighed Mrs. Blandings. Her husband felt he knew, but forbore to say.

Throughout the weeks, Mr. and Mrs. Blandings

and Mr. Simms had toiled onward and upward with the plans. "Mr. Simms is a tower of strength," Mrs. Blandings repeated over and over. It was comforting to the Blandings to realize how many times their architect must have gone through all their own vicissitudes with other would-be home builders; gone through them, and somehow come out, along with his clients, safely at the other end. When the ladies of the Historical Society finally presented, in attenuated form, the document designed to censure Mr. Blandings, Mr. Simms had been full of quiet sympathy and understanding; he had expressed himself eloquently on the worth and fate of the old Hackett house that neglect had doomed a decade ago, and rallied Mr. Blandings' courage nobly in the process. Whatever misfortune overtook the Blandings, Mr. Simms was somehow able to remember and discourse on something much worse that had happened to somebody else, who had, however, lived to tell the tale. Mountains might diminish and rivers change their course, but Mr. Simms remained the Blandings' one foundation.

The preliminary designs were still going slowly. This seemed to bother Mr. Simms scarcely at all. Mr. and Mrs. Blandings would change their minds a dozen times a week; old and dear ideas would suddenly become nauseous; new and vital ones, unconceived through the centuries, would need instant incorporation. Mr. Simms's cheerfulness

Mountains might diminish and rivers change their course, but Mr. Simms remained the Blandings' one foundation.

could not be dented. "It only costs us the price of an eraser to make our changes now," he would say as he obliterated one set of lines to make way for another. "Get them all out of your system early—they'll cost you real money as soon as the building starts." Mr. and Mrs. Blandings took this advice to heart; change after change occurred to them as the days wore on.

Mrs. Blandings came to realize, for example, that she had miscalculated the servant problem. She had begun by insisting that the country was where she wanted to come to *escape* from servants; she would do all her own housework and cooking, including the autumnal canning she was busy studying, and she would revel in it. But somehow the house was getting too big to be servantless, and thirty-one and one-half acres was—well, in a way it was too much land, rather than too little, when you thought of the spraying and the pruning and the haying and the weeding and the fertilizing that every inch of the top of Bald Mountain now appeared to need. So because the house was getting bigger than at first, it had to get a little bigger still; the Blandings would be in obvious need of hiring a couple: the man for outdoor work, his wife as cook and housekeeper. You couldn't just stick them in the attic, Mr. Simms warned; couples were getting pretty fussy. To get space for a small living room, bedroom, and bath at the kitchen end of the house called for quite a little ingenuity, but Mr. Simms supplied it after adding twelve feet to the house's long dimension.

It was in closets, perhaps, that Mrs. Blandings showed up most clearly as a woman of character. "All my life," she said, with an air of speaking for all womankind, "I've wanted to have enough closets." Now she had her chance, and she was resolved. Her proposal, on which she would retreat not one inch, called for two closets per bedroom, two in every hallway, one linen closet, one lingerie-and-shoe closet, a shallow closet in every bathroom, in addition to the medicine cabinet, to hold the overflow of proprietary remedies that was constantly accumulating in the Blandings household, one closet for outdoor clothes, two cleaning-materials closets (one per floor), one storage closet for wood, a closet for guests' wraps, a closet for folding chairs and card table, a canning closet and a laundry closet in the cellar, and a closet for flower vases in the back entryway. Mr. Blandings specified a liquor closet, with spring lock. It all added up to thirty-two closets, and Mrs. Blandings would brook no counterproposals except the elimination, if people were *really* sincere about saving space, of the liquor closet.

It turned out that Mr. Blandings viewed this closet as the one really indispensable storage compartment in the house, and its proposed elimination struck him as unfriendly. "Why don't we buy a blimp to commute in, and then you can have a closet for *it?*" he asked with the sort of heavy irony that particularly annoyed his wife. Mr. Simms, bending over his drafting board with elaborate attention until the disturbance passed, reflected that his old architectural school could profitably eliminate one semester of its long course in Shades and Shadows for the sake of

"It's beginning to look more like a $22,000 house every day," Mr. Simms observed to his clients.

teaching its students a few principles of how to deal with the domestic crises that a residential designer faced much more often than the declination of the sun. One evening he did a little multiplication and discovered that Mrs. Blandings' closets accounted for almost 3200 cubic feet on his conscientious plans.

"It's beginning to look more like a $22,000 house every day," he observed to his clients, and for the first time the word "mansion" was used in conversation—facetiously, of course.

The Blandings watched their house grow on the drafting board with warmth and pride. It was the embodiment of everything they had ever longed for, and it grew more perfect every day. Mr. Simms drew a new perspective sketch of it, with a garden and a few trees roughed in, and the Blandings looked at it for five minutes in wordless rapture that was a higher compliment than the most lavish praise. It looked like the old house in a way; it had the same clear, unadorned lines, the same solidity of proportion; a similarly massive chimney stack rose out of the broad, handsome roof; an unobtrusive overhang jutted out above the tops of the first-floor windows. Yet it was not the Old House, and owed little to it; it was a new house, spick, spandy, new on reinforced concrete sills that neither moth nor rust could corrupt, and a solid copper termite pan to keep every stick of wood clear of the contagious earth. The Blandings loved it so, a phrase developed on their lips that Mr. Simms could hear in his sleep: "While we're at it, we might as well—"

It was on this philosophy that a study for Mr. Blandings on the first floor passed from dream stuff to Sybaritic luxury to stark necessity within a short period of forty-eight hours. It was no easy matter to add one entire room to a ground plan already agreed upon, but a solution occurred to Mr. Simms one night, so deft and ingenious that he himself fell in love with it, and became emotionally incapable of further objections. This in turn made both necessary and possible the addition of a small cubicle, off the master bedroom, that Mrs. Blandings, in a moment of cuteness, referred to as a "sulking room"—something that would serve her either as dressing room or tiny study. The main part of the house thus now began to overbalance what was rapidly coming to be called the "service wing"; Mrs. Blandings had a happy notion for adding to its dignity and proportion by increasing the back vestibule space two feet to permit the addition of a little place for a sink and shelves where she could do her flower arranging. Mr. Blandings agreed to this in a flash, for the notion of the sink made it occur to him that a little built-in bar, placed off the living-room hall, and piped for hot and cold water, would add immeasurably to the house's whole feeling of hospitality—and who was Mr. Simms, who liked a snort now and then himself, to dispute the idea? It would permit, Mr. Blandings pointed out, the elimination of the liquor closet, after all.

On the second floor there was a bathroom right over the front entrance to the house, and although Mr. Blandings was willing to accept this as part of the same Cosmic Plan which had withheld water from Mr. Tesander until the 203rd foot, Mrs. Blandings fought it like a tigress and more than once embarrassed Mr. Blandings by the vividness with which she embodied her objections. There was no brooking her, Mr. Simms found; eventually, after a titanic struggle, he succeeded in getting the bathroom established in the rear without having to tear up all the plans and begin the design of another house altogether. But if Mrs. Blandings had won this battle, history might assess that it was precisely here she had lost the war: the house grew by another four feet of length. She felt no crisis; it was, it seemed to her, a blessing all around. With the additional space the bathroom providentially gave them, it was possible now to add a new access hall running clear through the house from front to back on the first floor. Mr. Simms was free to admit that this made a notable improvement in "circulation."

"I sometimes wonder if you people know what you're heading in for," Mr. Simms said one night as he packed up to go home. "Got your plans all laid for what bank you're going to rob?" But he and the Blandings were in a relaxed mood, with highballs in their hands that were full-bodied yet light, rich yet mild—and although it was not to be guessed from the advertisements of Mr. Blandings' fellow copywriters, the whisky involved possessed other virtues too, as the result of which not only Mr. Blandings but even his wife was lightly but effectually insulated from the deeper cares of life.

What was more, the warning note in Mr.

Simms's voice had become blunted from overuse—"He's a wonderful fellow, but he's always *harping* on something," Mr. Blandings had observed—and no longer served to convey admonition. The Blandings had *the* house of all the houses in the world they wanted; that the figure for cubage now stood at 69,000 was interesting but not alarming. It was a bad evening for warnings, anyway; a little earlier Mr. Tesander, God bless his lovely, beautiful soul, had run crash into nine gallons of water per minute at 297 feet and had telephoned the joyful news. There would be no need now to pursue this quest below the 300-foot level at which the cost per foot changed ominously from $4.50 to $6. Mr. Blandings, who had been mentally prepared to probe to 350 feet to get his water, was suddenly overjoyed to think that he had saved $313.50 by being able to stop at 297. It had been a lovely day; a thunderstorm had threatened from the west in the afternoon, but the clouds had vanished, and as Mr. Simms drove away from them the Blandings looked up into a night sky of late August that was powdery with stars.

It was apparent at last that the plans would soon be finished. Now that John Tesander was dismantling his rig and preparing to leave forever, Mr. Blandings no longer felt quite such an urge for the country. It occurred to him that if he clipped

Mr. Tesander had run crash into nine gallons of water and had telephoned the joyful news.

ten days from his vacation now he could more profitably return for another "week or two" later on. He began to lay plans for a fury of continuous fourteen-hour stints in New York whereby he could, with luck, turn out enough Knapp laxative copy to last sixty days, with updatings here and there as the Banton & Dascomb Media Department arranged its schedules for the winter. Mr. Banton was going to the Canadian Northwest; Mr. Dascomb was ensnarled in divorce proceedings of an awful complexity; the time would certainly be propitious for a little extra vacation if Mr. Blandings could just get that backlog of copy to last him until the really heavy season of intestinal stasis resumed around the first week in November.

The Knapp sales curves were going through the roof, Mr. Blandings discovered when he returned to the hot, disordered city; a seasonal down trend was actually in process of reversal, despite a thunderous denunciation by Dr. Morris Fishbein of the whole Knapp ethos, product, approach, and, above all, advertising. Mr. Blandings brewed himself pot after pot of coffee and sat before his typewriter in his empty, echoing apartment. After six days he had drafted twenty pieces of new Knapp copy, and made crude little pencil drawings on his younger daughter's school writing tablet for the benefit of the Banton & Dascomb art department. There were only some forty-five words to a piece of Knapp copy, so it was not the volume of output with which Mr. Blandings had to struggle. But he was a critical workman; he wrote and rewrote, and then re-rewrote over and over and over, like A. E. Housman agonizing over the quatrains of *A Shropshire Lad* but looking toward a wholly different end result. When he had finished he took a certain twisted pleasure in himself; what he had done was certainly horrible, but he was bound to admit that he had done it extremely well. After ten days of intensive creation and revision he took a Tuesday afternoon train back to Lansdale.

Things had gone well in his absence. "I always somehow seem to get more done when you're away," his wife said, not unkindly, but with point. "Mr. Simms and I went all the way to Seagate in his car to look at hardware and then we went together to see that International Wallboard Exposition near Blyfield. I got a lot of pointers."

Mrs. Blandings turned out to have got so many pointers that Mr. Blandings could not seem to catch up with her. It came over him that in the ten days he had been away his house had slipped out of his control. His feelings at this discovery were a blend of anxiety and irresponsibility in equal parts. He would find his wife and his architect discussing in familiar terms "the breezeway" of which he had never heard. Matters of cabinets, shelving, random-width floorboards, gutters, dry wells, olive-knuckle butts, flues, muntins, mullions, tiles, shakes, ranges, pitches, and reveals came at him in unexpected ways and from unexpected angles, and after a while Mr. Blandings gave up for good; he could not any longer stand the effect of his attempted interventions, which was merely that his wife and his architect would pause and look at him for fifteen seconds in silence before they resumed what he had interrupted. But he did not announce that he had given up, and Mr. Simms was therefore unaware of it; it seemed to him, in fact, that Mr. Blandings was becoming a somewhat more difficult client than before. That was due to the necessity Mr. Blandings now felt for approaching everything on a higher and more abstract plane; if the details had irretrievably escaped him, he would take refuge in the Higher Generalities, the Broader Picture, the Overall Content, as he had seen more than one founding businessman do as the day-by-day technicalities of the enterprise he had established slipped slowly from his grasp.

"When we build, let us think that we build for ever," John Ruskin once had written. Mr. Blandings heartily endorsed this view. The curse of America was jerry-building, he was eloquent in saying, and the Blandings' home, as it now lay all but finished on the drafting table, bore out the philosophies of quality and permanence. The floors were to be broad oak, the water lines red brass; the plumbing fixtures did not bear the trade-name of Sphinx for nothing; the incombustible shingles were the same as those developed to meet the wishes of Mr. Rockefeller for the restoration of Williamsburg; the hardware was to be supplied by the nearest thing to Benvenuto Cellini in Connecticut; the general run of lumber and glass was to be of Grade AA. That there were several grades of each that were higher in both quality and price was not known to Mr. Blandings—and *that,* thought Mr. Simms one night as he prepared for bed, was probably just as well.

One day it occurred to Mr. Blandings that his house on a mountaintop was beautifully situated to let him develop the hobby of amateur weather observation which had always appealed to him; he applied to the U. S. Weather Bureau for recognition as a volunteer observer, and shortly it was granted. Mr. Blandings thereupon plunged deep into half a dozen catalogues of anemometers, wet-and-dry-bulb thermometers, maximum-minimum thermometers, sunshine recorders, snow gauges, and recording wind-direction indicators, and immediately involved Mr. Simms in the redesign of a whole series of walls to include pipe chases which would carry the necessary wires from the instruments on the roof to the gauges in the master's study. It was getting late for this sort of thing, and Mr. Simms occasionally gave way to impatience.

"Why don't you just get the RFC to build the whole house?" he asked. "I think it's a project on the scale that would appeal to Jesse Jones."

"Isn't it a lot less expensive to plan it now than to have the idea later and rip everything apart?" Mr. Blandings demanded, nettled by Mr. Simms's unprecedented resort to satire. "This is the only chance I'm ever going to have in all my life to build a house, and shouldn't I have it the way I want it, within reasonable limits? God knows there's a lot of stuff we'd like to have that we've tossed out because it's too expensive. Didn't you say to make our changes now?" Mr. Simms had had to grant the point, and Mr. Blandings, too magnanimous to crush a fallen foe, had merely used a facial expression and a gesture of Latin economy and vividness to convey to Mr. Simms an unanswerable "Well, then?"

But Mr. Simms's petulance had its effect; Mr. and Mrs. Blandings suddenly announced that they would present no further new ideas. It was wonderfully, gorgeously possible to go on improving a house, dreaming up new spaces, new ideas, new gadgets, forever, but prudence dictated that now they should stop. It seemed too bad, but as the years went by they could doubtless add an improvement here or there, once they had lived in the house for a couple of years and, as with a marriage, discovered the unexpected quirks, the hidden flaws, that no period of courtship, however long, could properly and completely reveal. "There'll be bugs in it, all right," the Blandings had assured their friends the Grovers one evening at dinner. "We know that. It's impossible to imagine how anybody could have been more conscientious and far-sighted than Andy Simms, but you can't foresee everything. We're prepared for the bugs; let 'em come; we've done our best. Remember how the Longwells built that $75,000 palace of theirs and their architect forgot the chimney?"

Mr. Blandings and his auditors dissolved into laughter at the Longwells' unhappy designer, but Mrs. Blandings looked suddenly serious.

"Heavens!" she said, a hand to her cheek. "Chimney! Lightning rods! *Mr. Simms has forgotten lightning rods on the chimney!* I'd no more think of living in a house in the country without lightning rods than I would a house without plumbing."

When Mr. Simms was faced with his oversight, he remarked, with a trace of the same satiric tendency that had recently come to mark him, that he had also forgotten to buy the Blandings' china for them; his intention seemed to be to emphasize to Mrs. Blandings that there were matters connected with a house that did not lie in the province of the architect and that here was one of them; if the Blandings wished a lightning protective system, they were welcome to it, and he would even put them in touch with a—the phrase suggested to Mr. Blandings an old dirty story, long forgotten—lightning-rod salesman. If they insisted that he draw some lines on his plans indicating rods and cables and ground connections, he would be glad to, but it would cost the Blandings ten per cent of the cost of the installation and he, Mr. Simms, didn't think it would be worth it to them.

This was the first remark about money or compensation that had ever passed between architect and client, Mr. Blandings realized, and somehow he felt sober about it.

Then, one evening, Mr. Simms arose from his portable drafting board with a happy sigh of conclusion. One phase of home building was finished at last, he announced; another was now about to begin. He would go now into a monastic seclusion with a draftsman helper, to set to on the actual *working* drawings. What the Blandings had seen so far were the mere preliminaries; a sort of set of memoranda agreed to between the Blandings and himself. To the Blandings, he explained, they conveyed everything; to a contractor, they would not even begin to provide the information needed for study and estimate. The specifications his clients and he had been tossing lightly about, from memory, from Sweet's monumental building catalogue, or out of fantasy undefiled, must now be reduced to the coldest and hardest literal fact. He shook hands, told the Blandings it had all been great fun so far, and made ready to vanish out of their lives. If they took his advice, said Mr. Simms, they'd forget all about their house for several weeks. It would be that long before he could see them again, anyway, and it was his feeling that the Blandings were a little stale on residence design.

How nicely this is turning out, thought the Blandings. Labor Day was almost at hand, and the Blandings' children were momentarily due home from summer camp. Mrs. Blandings had before her an orgy of reoutfitting for their new school term, and other responsibilities connected with September. She would go back to New York for a week or two, collect and process the children, and then, before school opened, bring the whole family back again to the cottage at Bald Mountain's foot, to spend the balance of Mr. Blandings' hoarded vacation in the flamingly gorgeous days of early autumn.

It all worked out with a neatness to which the Blandings were not usually accustomed, and which Mr. Blandings took as the best possible augury for their future. Betsy and Joan had put Dymaxion houses, Stout Mobile Homes, and Zamboni Power Units even further behind them than the previous summer; they had regressed now to the purest and most servile totem worship of the architectural past. Betsy had read Kelly's *Early Connecticut Architecture* four times through during the summer, to place her on the plane of importance she hoped for with Mr. Simms; Joan had fallen deep under the spell of some unidentified John Deweyite counselor at camp, and was so full of the doctrine of learning by doing that the geology, mineralogy, and botany of Bald Mountain supplied her with every intellectual need. Both children, seeing "Betsy's Room" and "Joan's Room" in Mr. Simms's best architectural script on the plans became wholly proprietary and abandoned themselves in the evenings to interior decoration in the best manner of Lady Mendl. Everything seemed to be on a very clear track indeed.

When Mr. Simms emerged from his seclusion into the Blandings' lives again he had with him a set of tracings and blueprints that floored his clients flat. They were bound by a wooden rod into something the size and thickness of a book of wallpaper samples ("Heavens, *wallpaper,*" Mrs. Blandings murmured, and rushed to make a note), and they were like nothing the Blandings had ever seen before. The simple drawings they had watched grow on the drafting board were superseded now by framing plans, wiring diagrams, and detail sheets; by incomprehensible blueprints labeled "Section at A-A." The plans and elevations had become so dense with dimensioning that the Blandings could scarcely discover where their rooms had vanished. Along with the innumerable blueprints there was a set of specifications the thickness of a Chicago telephone directory.

It was now, Mr. Simms informed his clients in a sepulchral voice, time to ask for bids.

IX

The Financial Angle

John Tesander had long since gone away, but Mr. Blandings still missed him. Just after Labor Day his bill arrived, inscribed in a lovely copperplate, and Mr. Blandings wondered if the same stout fists that had swung the sledge and guided the whipping drill cable could have inscribed these precise, delicate strokes. It was quite possible, he thought; Mr. Tesander was one of those people who could not do anything badly.

The bill was for $1336.50. Mr. Blandings jumped when he saw the figure, but 297 feet at $4.50 a foot came to that, at the precise penny. There were no ingenious extras, no stretches of the agreement for additional this or undiscussed that. Mr. Blandings paid it with the first pleasure at disbursal he had so far experienced. But the neatly capped casing pipe which was the only evidence that Mr. Tesander had left behind him of his hard and now invisible toil gave him a sudden thought as he looked at it. He went scurrying to Mr. Simms's neat plans—the comprehensible ones, that he had watched in the making—and there confirmed a suspicion that might well, he reflected, have dawned upon him before. On the drawings of the cellar, a careful arrow and the words “From Pump House” in architectural lettering made him realize that there was a gap between where Mr. Tesander’s labors left off and a plumber’s could begin. The gap would have to be filled, and only Mr. Blandings could fill it. It consisted of a deep-well pump and a snugly buried water tank beside it.

Mr. Blandings simply did not know whether to be angry or dejected. For the second time, a vital matter in the domain of water supply had all but slipped his mind. Was it merely that he was becoming an utter, vacuous fool, with a simian knack of writing advertising copy for a tonnage laxative, and no other uses or capacities whatever? Mr. Blandings sadly guessed so. But—*damn it!*—there was the exit of the main soil line on Mr. Simms’s plans, and *it* was marked, “To Septic Tank, See Specifications.” Lo and behold, the specifications drooled on for two pages about the septic tank and its connections—it must be lined with pitch, it must have a vitrified tile header, capped vent tiles, shear gates, and be bedded in straw, cinders, and gravel. It sounds good enough to eat, Mr. Blandings thought disgustedly. If architects put septic tanks into their contract specifications, why the hell didn’t they put in pumps, and water-storage tanks, and the big copper tubes that would lead from pump house to cellar, and the trenches that would have to be dug for them? He looked to the heavens for answer

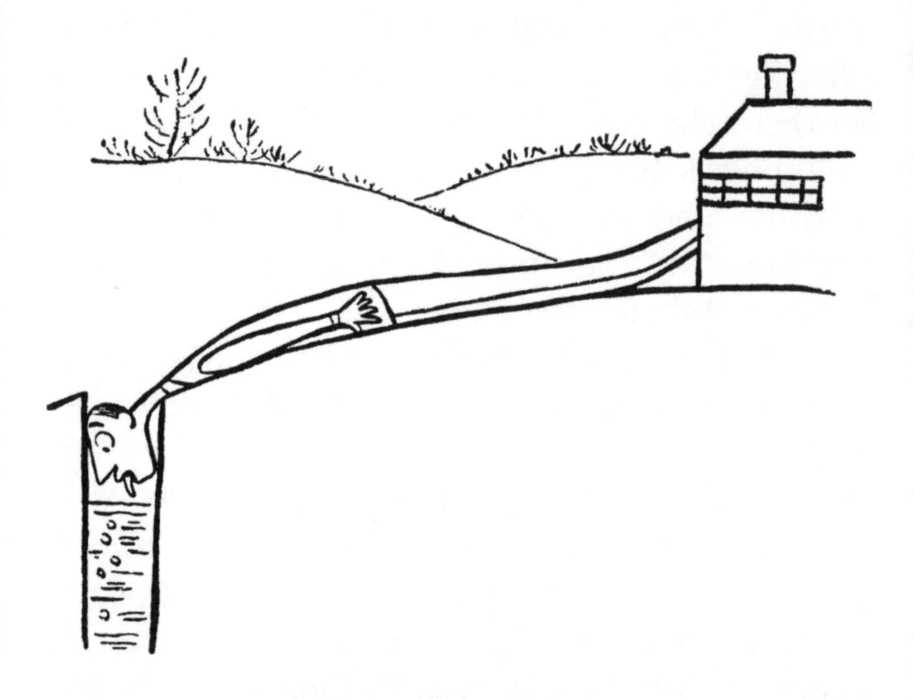

There was a gap between where Mr. Tesander's labors left off and a plumber's could begin, and only Mr. Blandings could fill it.

and received none. Instead, the heavens suggested that he had better not postpone any longer the business of borrowing the money on which he was to build his house, much though he disliked to think that this time was at last inexorably here. At an early opportunity, the heavens added, he had better consult Mr. Anson Dolliver, President of the Lansdale National Bank.

Mr. Blandings had had the foresight, a year earlier, to open a checking account in Mr. Dolliver's bank: he had kept his balance there at a level he was sure a country bank would consider opulent. Mr. Dolliver had been cordiality itself the day Mr. Blandings first made himself a depositor; he had come out from behind the glassed enclosure that served as his office and introduced himself; he'd known who Mr. Blandings was, he explained, and hoped this chance would come. He had complimented Mr. Blandings on his astuteness in buying the particular thirty-one and one-half acres that were his, and not a square foot more. "Took the very heart out of old Eph Hackett's land up there, 's what you did, like all you city people coming up here and dipping off mountaintops for yourselves."

He put just the right blend of admiration and ruefulness into his voice, and Mr. Blandings had felt himself swelling slightly despite his attempted restraints. Mr. Dolliver had gone on to discuss the changing community his bank had the privilege of serving. He remarked that although some townsfolk resented the intrusion of city dwellers into a community that had been so distinctly *sui generis* for two hundred years, he, Mr. Dolliver, did not share this parochial view, particularly with the fine type of outlander represented by Mr. Blandings. He had ended with a contemptuous *sotto voce* reference to Mrs. Prutty, the significance of which was not to dawn on Mr. Blandings for some time to come.

This happy initial conversation was repeated at

regular intervals; the pattern grew more cordial and the occasions more frequent, until it got to be that cashing a $25 check on a Saturday morning to buy the week-end groceries and liquor often took Mr. Blandings as much as half an hour. Mr. Dolliver invariably ended such a chat with the warm suggestion, "If we can ever help you out, up there on the hill, just let us know."

"Well," said Mr. Blandings to himself as he drove to Lansdale Town on a Saturday morning, "now you can help me, up there on the hill, Mr. Dolliver, so here I come to let you know." He did not particularly like Mr. Dolliver, but perhaps he should learn to, for he was certainly now about to commit himself solidly to Mr. Dolliver's bank. Mr. Blandings envisioned from Mr. Dolliver cordiality in the extreme, the proffer of a fine cigar, the suggestion of a leisurely lunch at the pleasant restaurant up the tree-lined street, and an open line of credit at a nominal rate.

What he encountered was nothing like that at all.

"So now you want some money for that enterprise of yours up there," said Mr. Dolliver, with a curious stress, that Mr. Blandings did not like, on the word "enterprise." He bit off the end of a cigar for himself and spat daintily in Mr. Blandings' direction, but proffered nothing. He seemed puzzled and displeased that Mr. Blandings had brought up such a topic as money; as if Mr.

Blandings were making a presumption on his importance as a depositor. Mr. Blandings began to murmur something about a need for cash and instantly loathed himself for its tentative, apologetic, and defensive quality.

"Why, great grief," said Mr. Dolliver, breaking in, "we're loaned full up to our legal limit right now; have been for longer'n I could tell you. Love to help you out, but—" He left the sentence unfinished, while Mr. Blandings dangled in mid-air. Then he added, as if a bright solution to an unusual problem had just occurred to him: "My brother's the president of the savings bank across the hall. *He* might be able to do something for you. . . ."

Mr. Blandings, thoroughly shaken, but unwilling to discuss with anybody the complete alteration in Mr. Dolliver's personality, lest he reveal his own considerable naïveté in financial affairs, had three separate conversations with the savings-bank brother, at the end of which the second-string Dolliver admitted that there might be circumstances under which his bank would make a $10,000 mortgage loan to Mr. Blandings at six and one-half per cent. Feeling like Lord Keynes at the end of a tough mission, Mr. Blandings said that he had hoped for more money at less rate, and the road-company Dolliver had responded with a concise lecture on the risks involved in rural real estate that Mr. Blandings wished he had been able to think up for himself a year ago.

"What you're planning, Mr. Blanders," he said, his finger tips together and his head on one side, "is a gentleman's estate, if you don't mind my calling it that, and a very fine ornament to this modest community. That is just my point. The amount of this bank's participation that I could recommend to my directors is limited by my knowledge that if any, that is to say, contraction were to take place in your affairs, there would be so few people hereabouts who would be in a position to take over from you, if I am making myself clear."

Mr. Blandings swallowed; it was obvious that his financial bargaining power in Lansdale was not what he had thought it. He contented himself by wondering aloud how soon he might have Mr. Dolliver's accommodation on the terms laid down, since his bids were almost due, and he hoped to begin breaking ground very soon.

Mr. Dolliver snapped forward in his chair, his bland manner evaporated like a breath of ether in a gale. "You want this money for *construction?*" he asked, in a tone that made Mr. Blandings feel that he had sought to procure a criminal abortion from an archbishop. Mr. Blandings said he did, in a voice he tried to make firm.

"You've had me at a misapprehension," said Mr. Dolliver. "This bank *never* makes construction loans. If that's your situation and you have some government bonds, I think my brother in the commercial bank across the hall could work out something very satisfactory for you."

It was at this moment that the original Dolliver strolled across the hall, intent on a word with his brother. He checked himself when he saw Mr. Blandings rising to take his leave, but too late to avoid acknowledging his presence.

"Well," he said, "get it all fixed up?"

Suddenly Mr. Blandings began to tremble with rage. Mr. Dolliver was not the first member of the community to attempt rape on him while affecting to be a detached observer of the human comedy, but somehow he was the least lovable.

"We didn't get a Goddamn thing fixed up," said Mr. Blandings, "and you don't need to ask. I don't know what the hell you and your brother do in this bank that a pig couldn't do better."

A savings bank is designed for hush and Mr. Blandings' voice would have carried well at Ebbets Field. He could hear it echo and re-echo between the marble floor and the high plaster ceiling, but he could do nothing about it.

"You can take your tin-pot bank and shove the assets down your throats two bits at a time," said Mr. Blandings in what was partly a yell and partly a sob. "This is the only place within thirty-five miles where anybody can cash a check and that makes you two manure-covered hicks think you're the De Beers Diamond Syndicate. All I want from you is a check for the balance in my checking account and after I get it I wouldn't come back here if you had a pay toilet."

This was incredible.

"Walter!" cried the older Dolliver.

An elderly clerk in a lightweight gray coat rushed to Mr. Dolliver's side, as if to prevent an assassination.

"Get me a cashier's check for the balance in the Blandings account, Walter," said Mr. Dolliver. "If any checks outstanding show up send them back marked No Account, and don't forget to deduct the service charges."

He turned back to Mr. Blandings. "Go give your account back to Winthrop W. Aldrich," he said with heavy scorn. "The Chase is only the second largest bank in the country now, so they'll appreciate your helping them out of a hole. We got along fine here without your class of business for a long time, and I guess we can do it again."

When it was all over and he stood outside the bank's plate-glass window, his cashier's check crumpled to a soggy ball in his hand, Mr. Blandings' rage began to turn to guilt, and the guilt to fear. He had made a scene in a public place; he was self-humiliated. He would go down in local history as the barbaric despoiler who had first torn down a sacred shrine on a cloud-wreathed mountaintop, and then vomited on the altar of the cult's high priest, Capital $250,000, Surplus $250,000. He could picture his tombstone in the local burying ground he always passed on his way from Bald Mountain to Lansdale Town. "James H. Blandings," it would say; "known as 'The Wretched'; unwept, unhonored, unsung."

He could scarcely tell a coherent story to Mrs. Blandings that evening when he settled down to try, and it was several days before his memories ceased to be so turbulent that he could not sit still in his easy chair. After a while he was able to begin hunting for a silver lining, and presently he found it. It had not been pleasant to deal with the Dollivers, but he could at least congratulate himself that here was one episode that had not cost him any money. He merely did not have his loan.

X
Bids

Mr. Blandings was in a state of what seemed to be permanent depression, mixed with alternations of lethargy and irritation. That a Christmas was coming in several months which would doubtless bring him a plump bonus to signalize one of the best years in the history of cathartics did not buoy him up. He had been a man, he reflected, not only of good professional standing, but of substance, in a mild way. He had accumulated some $20,000, saved out of his own earnings, and the knowledge (he had thought) of how to come by more. But the greater part of the $20,000 had now been swallowed up or pre-empted by the demands of real-estate ownership, and still he had no house. He had not even the beginnings of a house, unless Mr. John Tesander's well could be counted.

What was more, he was a stranger, and alone. The clash with the Dollivers had illuminated something for him with a lightning stroke: in the midst of the bucolic loveliness where he had wanted to live in peace and harmony with nature and his fellows, he was disliked. He did not think it was anything about him personally, although of course he could be wrong. He even doubted that it had anything, or anything much, to do with the tearing down of the Old House. It was just that he was an outlander. He could wear overalls, or dress in mail-order clothes, or part his hair down the middle, until kingdom come, and it would make no difference. He could live in a cow barn until all the perfumes of Araby were powerless to lighten the smell of wet leaves and manure, but the natives of Lansdale County would still know him for an alien, forever. He would still be a City Man on masquerade, a slicker taken in trespass.

He tried to remember what chain of circumstances, what association of emotions, had ever persuaded him in the first place that he wanted a house in the country, a home of his own. But he was in such a state of lethargic confusion that he could somehow not trace the evil river on which he was now floating, oarless and alone, back to anything that could be called its source. Was Mrs. Blandings responsible? Mr. Blandings sort of thought so, but could not exactly recall. What was it that who had said to whom, when, and under what circumstances that had planted this seed in his bosom that he wanted to be one of the Builders of America, a man and citizen and householder whose way of life was Freedom, who could look all the swollen landlords of the Western world straight in the eye and tell them where to go? He thought of all the advertisements he had ever read from the pens of all his brother copywriters; the little booklets of the nation's savings banks and their hymns about the joys of Ownership—with half-tones of a placid man reading while a placid woman sewed and a placid child played beside a placid hearth—all order, convention, calm; the unanticipated and accidental fleeing elsewhere to happen. He thought of the rich bogusness of a four-color linoleum ad, wherein the cellar of a Korkomatic Home combined the calm dignity of a crypt with the warmth of an Andalusian patio, and the house functioned with the unassailable silence and good order of a spinning top. *God damn it,* why were his honest, earnest, yearning efforts to create such an El Dorado for the Blandings family so saddled and hampered and addled by every conceivable mischance and marplot within 500 miles?

He had not dared to confess to Mrs. Blandings that as a sort of maraschino cherry on top of the fermented banana split that was his life (Mr. Blandings' illustrative figures were beginning to take on a wildly inappropriate quality that might have alarmed a psychiatrist) he had totally mislaid every legal paper that attested to his ownership of the thirty-one and a half acres of Bald Mountain. Not that it mattered; not that he would care very much any more if it *did* matter. Still, he experienced the same sort of tiny, nagging torture that would beset him when, as happened once in a while, he would know that he had lighted a cigarette and placed it, idly burning, in an ash tray, and then search the house only to find every such receptacle from cellar to garret empty and gleaming. . . . *Where were those papers? Where was that Deed? Where was that Purchase Agreement? Where was that Survey and Survey Map? Where was that Certificate of Title?*

"I think you ought to go away someplace and get a good rest," said Mrs. Blandings from her corner. "You're looking all drawn and tired. What you need is a little vacation."

"I'm *on* vacation," said Mr. Blandings. "Don't you remember that I went back to the city and did eight weeks' work in ten days so that I could be up here when the bids were due? Why else would I be here now, instead of in New York?"

"I forgot," said Mrs. Blandings.

On that instant Mr. Blandings remembered where his missing papers were. They were in the safe-deposit box in Mr. Dolliver's bank that Mr. Blandings had rented over a year ago for their express safekeeping. There was no way to get them out except by crossing Mr. Dolliver's threshold and marching down thirty echoing feet of marble, past Mr. Dolliver's glass-enclosed desk, and the staring eyes of a half-dozen of his apprentices in usury. He had sworn he would not be found dead in Mr. Dolliver's bank, but maybe that was where he *would* be found dead. He had better go away, as Mrs. Blandings was suggesting; indeed he had; if he were destined never to return, well . . .

Mr. Simras arrived on a Saturday morning, looking a little constricted about the mouth, but brisk. "We've got all our bids," he said. "I've summarized them on the top sheet."

Mr. Blandings opened the Manila folder and leaped upward as from a bayonet thrust through the chair bottom.

"Jesus H. Mahogany Christ!" cried Mr. Blandings, and let the folder slip from his grasp. Mrs. Blandings, who had borne the younger Blandings daughter without anesthetics on the grounds that she did not wish to miss the experience, picked up the sheets as they slithered to the floor. She bent a level gaze on them and read:

Estimates — Blandings Job — Bald Mountain

Antonio Doloroso, Builders	$32,117.00
Caries & Plumline	34,265.00
Julius Akimbo & Co.	37,500.00
Zack, Tophet & Payne	28,920.50
John Retch & Sons	30,852.00

"There are a couple of things to be noticed from this," said Mr. Simms, speaking in an even, level, slightly rapid voice. "In the first place, Julius Akimbo obviously doesn't want the job or he

"We've got all our bids," said Mr. Simms.

wouldn't have put in any round-figure bid that size. As for that bid from Zack, Tophet & Payne, I wouldn't touch it with a ten-foot pole. They have a reputation for bidding low and then loading on the extras. That would leave John Retch low man, and I'd be happy to see him get the job; I've worked with him, and he's my idea of a sound, honest builder. Even so, I think we'll have to go to work and cut some of our costs."

This, Mr. Blandings thought in a blurred sort of way, was putting it mildly. He thought of the $20,000 assumption with which he and his wife had started out and wondered again, as best he could, why everything was turning out so differently from the way he and Mrs. Blandings used to dream of it in their snug city apartment. Later in the day, after Mr. Simms had quietly withdrawn, Mr. Blandings sat down with a pencil and a piece of paper and wrote down everything he could think of that related to the costs of Ownership and Freedom. When he added the Retch bid to a long column of figures preceding it, there arose to confront him from his scratch pad a hideous figure somewhat in excess of $45,000.

The cost-cutting job began that afternoon, early. What Mr. Blandings now discovered was that you could cut the cost of a $31,000 house *somewhat*—at the sacrifice of everything you wanted most—but there was no way on earth to cut a $31,000 house down to a $21,000 house any more than there was a way of making marmosets out of a zebra by trimming down and rearranging the zebra. A $31,000 house belonged to one species; a $21,000 house to another. And yet there seemed nothing to do but try.

It was slow, dispiriting work. Moreover, some things were irreversible: it was no longer possible to shrink the house by restoring the fatal bathroom to its flaunting position over the front door; too much else had altered in the meantime, and you could no more reverse the growth process of the house that way than you could force an adolescent back into last year's clothes even by the inhumanity of denying him food.

What was worse, Mrs. Blandings was lending only the most fainthearted efforts to cost reduction, and even the rectitudinous Mr. Simms was not killing himself with exertions. He had warned his clients every step of the way that they were insisting upon a house not specified in their budget, and they had given lip service to his cautions and gone their headlong way. Now Mr. Simms, himself somewhat carried away by the previous airiness of his clients, had achieved a creation of which he was justly proud, and he would have been notably more than human had he been willing to throw it into the fire and start again. When Mr. Blandings proposed to him that the plan be kept precisely as it was but all dimensions be shrunk fifteen per cent, Mr. Simms had shuddered as though a cold, rough wind had set the silken whiskers of John Ruskin in total disarray. When Mr. Blandings turned to his wife and renewed a line of attack upon the closets, it was only to discover that Mrs. Blandings, like Eugene Aram before her, had closed her mind and clasped it with a clasp.

Yet something had to be done, and more than something. The house could not be abandoned.

For one thing, although Mr. Simms had made only one brief, elliptical remark about money, and had seemed willing to go on designing the Blandings' house forever, Mr. Blandings was aware that the standard architect's fee for residential design was, according to the procedures of the American Institute of Architects, ten per cent of the cost of the house—and God knew that if anybody had ever earned $3100, it was Mr. Simms. Manifestly he could not now be asked to design a new $21,000 house and receive only a $2100 fee; if Mr. Blandings were now to conceive another and less expensive house, he would owe Mr. Simms for the design of two houses, not one. With Mr. Funkhauser in the past that would mean three architects' fees, but only one house, if that. It would be delightful, Mr. Blandings thought, to abandon Bald Mountain utterly and forever; to return to the city and move a final, cautious ten blocks farther north, and die of old age in a rented apartment in the East Eighties. But he could not do that now; he had reached and passed the crucial mark known, in the poetic language of the air navigator, as the Point of No Return.

Mr. Blandings, accepting the analogy, flew on; through thunder, lightning, and in rain. Despite all obstacles, some deflation of the house did set in: bronze casements changed to steel; their cross section diminished in weight not once but several times. Red-brass piping first became yellow brass, then galvanized iron. The roofing specifications came down in the world. The project for insulating the house against the summer heat and winter cold with billowy rock-wool batts from ridge to sills was reduced to rock-wool to be blown in after the walls were all but sealed, and it would stop at the eaves at that. The plumbing fixtures became notably less Pompeian. A whole flagged terrace disappeared. Mr. Retch, informed that the job would be his, submitted a schedule of reductions based upon altered specifications.

No one had any heart for any of it. It depressed Mr. Blandings still further to observe that the elimination of the terrace, on which he had already, in anticipation, sat in the cool of the evening and invited his soul, saved him, on Mr. Retch's figures, only $172.50. "If I was *adding* the terrace it wouldn't cost me a cent less than $700," said Mr. Blandings, savagely. But he said it to himself, for he no longer had anyone to talk to. He was being cheated, he was being bilked, he was being made a fool of, but he could not find the villain, because everyone was a villain—his wife, Mr. Simms, the local bank, John Retch and his bastard sons, the Stoop Biological Laboratories, the Lansdale Historical Society, Mr. Perlasky, Mr. Funkhauser, Mr. Apollonio, Ephemus Hackett, and the real-estate man—all, all had made him the

He could not find the villain, because everyone was a villain.

butt and victim of a huge conspiracy, clever and cruel.

"There!" he heard Mrs. Blandings say to Mr. Simms a fortnight later. "We've got Mr. Retch's figures down to $26,991.17. That's more like it."

"What's more like *what?*" Mr. Blandings snarled, the milk of human kindness acidophilus within him.

"I think," said Mr. Simms, tactfully, "we've

pared it down as far as it will go. It's more money than you started out to spend, but you're getting a fine house, if I do say so myself, and one that would be pretty easy to resell someday, if you ever had to, or had a mind to. Cut it down any more and you'd be getting into false economies. Retch is an honest builder and that's about what your house will cost you—*if* you don't start getting into a lot of extras with him."

With one voice, Mr. and Mrs. Blandings assured Mr. Simms that there would be *no* extras. Far, far off in outer space, the Gods of Residential Construction offered a chirruping laugh.

Mr. Blandings' ego, scarred by forces too vast for him to identify, was powerfully restored a fortnight later on his visit to the big, impressive savings bank in the industrial city of Seagate, nearest metropolis to Lansdale Town. Thither Mr. Blandings and Bill Cole had gone to seek the mortgage which had come to naught with the local bank. The big bank and its friendly officers gave back to Mr. Blandings his sense of security, balance, and sanity, missing for a long and serious time. The chief mortgage officer had congratulated him on Mr. Simms's excellent plans; spoken highly, from personal knowledge, of the Blandings-Hackett acreage, and looked with satisfaction on Mr. Blandings' statement of salary and financial position. In no more than an hour's conversation the bank had agreed to advance Mr. Blandings $18,000 at five per cent, the loan to be amortized over twenty years, anticipation of repayments permitted. That fell far short of Mr. Blandings' commitments, but Bill Cole had advised against asking for a larger mortgage. To make up the balance, Mr. Blandings would have to hock a large chunk of the Banton & Dascomb stock he had been permitted to acquire; there was no other way to get his dream house built and functioning. But *of course,* said the bank in conclusion, the loan would be a construction loan; Mr. Blandings could have access to cash as soon as the bank's title attorneys had completed their search on the Old Hackett Property.

This last puzzled Mr. Blandings but did not disturb him. "I thought we'd done that," he said to Bill Cole as they left the bank together. "What did I pay old Judge Quarles $125 for when I bought the property from Hackett in the first place?"

Bill Cole explained that that had been a title search, all right. "It would have satisfied the local bank if you'd been able to do business with them," he said. "But Seagate-Proletarian is a pretty big institution; they have $5,000,000 out in mortgages in a hundred communities besides yours, and they have to have their own guarantees and satisfactions, naturally. It won't amount to much. Their title attorneys are Barratry, Lynch & Virgo; they'll soak you $250, but it'll be worth it to have their stamp of approval if you were ever to resell, for example."

This idea of resale that seemed to crop up so perpetually in Bill Cole's discussions of Bald Mountain no longer had the jangling effect upon Mr. Blandings' nerves that once it had had when all the world was new. Now, in fact, he found it rather soothing; there was still a Way Out, after all.

"They'll really do a good job, will they?" he asked.

"You bet they will," said Bill Cole. "Not that it's difficult. The clue to the whole business is to send a man up to check the county records, and go over all the details of everything in the past with old Judge Quarles."

"Old Judge Quarles died last spring," said Mr. Blandings. "The whole town closed down the afternoon of his funeral."

"Oh," said Bill Cole, and then, after a moment's pause, "well, he didn't take his records with him, I guess."

On a crisp autumnal day the steam shovel arrived. Bill Cole was still fussing with the innumerable papers that seemed to be involved in a contract for the building of a house, but Mr. John Retch had allowed that he was not a man to stand on ceremony and wanted to get his shovel working while he could. He and Mr. Simms were both present for the ground breaking, and Mrs. Blandings was delighted with the rugged honesty and loud good humor of their contractor—"A rough diamond with a heart of gold," she averred. They had asked him down to their cottage for a drink before he left to tour his other jobs, and his mixture of forthrightness and embarrassed deference in the Blandings' rented sitting room had been simply charming. He had treated the Blandings girls as young ladies, not as children, and had professed admiration of Betsy's architectural lore. She had pronounced him "cuter than William Bendix," a remark her puzzled mother took to mean endorsement.

Mrs. Blandings was also happy that Mr. Blandings seemed himself again, as indeed he did. Any man who could raise $18,000 in an hour's conversation with one of the biggest savings banks in the East had certainly no call to be as jumpy about his finances and general position in life as Mr. Blandings could now see, looking back on it all, he had permitted himself to become. The $10,000-odd he would have to borrow on his Banton & Dascomb stock was just about the net of his burden; that was one way of looking at it. Everything else—and there had been a lot of unexpected things, let us not deceive ourselves—everything else had been cash that he would have spent on something else if it hadn't been for the house; something silly, probably, and certainly not with all the solid, unalterable permanence of a home for his wife and children, forever. He could see himself before his own fireplace, successfully home after a Yale-Harvard game (Yale 28, Harvard 0), impressing his daughters' young admirers with the breadth and sanity of his views on a variety of topics. They would have formed the habit of calling him "sir," and the hair at his temples would be gray, but in his heart there would be serenity. . . .

As for the mortgage, that was the bank's worry, not his; they were going to get five per cent for their worrying, and if they were satisfied, so was he. A five per cent loan, running for twenty years—why, that meant the bastards would double their money on him; for giving him $18,000 now they would eventually get back from him $36,000 over the next twenty years, minus the little sums of compound interest in reverse. No; that was not the way to look at it; the way to look at it was that he would pay only $900 worth of interest in his first year, which would decrease every year as he amortized his loan. That was pretty piffling when you considered it as the rent on a twelve-room house with four baths and the loveliest mountain view in all the world. Someday, a swimming pool could go in that natural hollow below the sun porch, and be fed by the brook; you could swim in the Goddamn water, anyway, if you couldn't drink it. But that was something to think about a couple of years from now; either before the tennis court or after it, he wasn't sure which. It would probably be nice to do the pool first, because then, when you had the tennis court you could go in for a cool dip after you'd finished a few strenuous sets, whereas if you did the tennis court first—

"I wonder why the steam shovel isn't working," said Mrs. Blandings. It had been half an hour now since she had heard its snortings come drifting down the hill.

"He's been at it for five hours," said Mr. Blandings, rousing himself and speaking of the villainous-looking man who had turned out to be Mr. Retch's excavating subcontractor. "Let's see what our hole in the ground looks like."

Hand in hand, like happy children, the Blandings climbed the hill—*their* hill, as Mrs. Blandings put it now. The evil days were behind them. The delays had been galling; the mistakes costly. The experience had been bitterly won, but won it was. Their plans were perfect, their money was in sight, and now, thank God, *work* had at last begun. Nothing was so cozy, Mrs. Blandings thought, as the sight of workmen plying their trade on behalf of a home, where one day soon a woman and her breadwinner and the children of their love would dwell in peace and harmony together.

On the Blandings' building site, yesterday had seen only some stakes with stout lines of mason's twine stretched between them to mark the boundaries of the excavation. It had been exciting enough to watch the men lay out the dimensions on the ground; now it was doubly exciting to see the earth heaved and turned to receive Mr. Simms's and the Blandings' Masterpiece. At one corner, Mr. Giuseppe Zucca's steam shovel rested unevenly on its elephantlike treads. In the south portion of the staked-out ground it had dug a hole, gratifyingly sharp, that went down six feet at the edges. Toward the north side, the excavation was ragged and uneven, and while the shovel operator sat in his cab and smoked, three men with spades were at work with the earth. The noise that came forth from their instruments was the same sort of noise the Blandings were accustomed to hear through the windows of their city apartment on a winter morning when a light fall of snow was being scraped from the pavements beneath them. As the men worked, Mr. and Mrs. Blandings could see growing the outlines of what appeared to be a colossal ossified whale.

"Looka that," said Mr. Zucca.

"Boulder?" inquired Mr. Blandings, genially.

"Boulder!" said Mr. Zucca, in derision. "Atsa no boulder, atsa *ledge.* We go home now, come back next week, start blasting, keep on blasting plenty, yes, *sir.* One thing you never got to worry your house settle any, sitting on granite, no, *sir.*" He bellowed an incomprehensible command and all

There was a flaw in the title.

work stopped. "Bust a part on the shovel, very first day, when the bucket hit the ledge," he said disgustedly. "*Bad* luck."

When he got back to his fireside, Mr. Blandings looked up Mr. Retch's estimates on excavation. The job was to be done for $500 flat, except for the proviso, "If rock encountered, removal by blasting at $.24 per cubic foot; dynamite and caps extra." It had not seemed much, but the nature of cubic equations had once before eluded Mr. Blandings. This time he took pencil and paper, to discover that an excavation sixty feet long, twenty-eight feet wide, and six feet deep contained 10,080 cubic feet.

Mr. Blandings was just beginning to wonder what sizable fraction of this figure should be multiplied by $.24, and how much a stick of dynamite cost (he might any day want some for himself, he mused, his sense of joy fading with the sunlight), when the telephone rang. With a leaden hand Mr. Blandings placed the receiver at an ear which did not wish to hear. Bill Cole's voice greeted him with what Mr. Blandings instantly knew to be false cheer.

"I don't want you to fly off the handle, Jim," Bill's voice said, "but there's a little hitch."

"What kind of a hitch?" Mr. Blandings heard himself ask.

"I've just been talking to Barratry, Lynch's man, Hank Pugh, who's doing your legal job for the bank," said Bill Cole.

"And so what?" said Mr. Blandings.

"There's a flaw in the title," said Mr. Blandings' attorney.

Book Two

XI
Autumn Crocus

After size and weight, the Power of architecture may be said to depend on the quantity of its shadow; the reality of its works and the use and influence they have in the daily life of men . . . require of it that it should express a kind of human sympathy, by a measure of darkness as great as there is in human life: and that as the great poem and great fiction generally affect us most by the majesty of their masses of shade, and cannot take hold upon us if they affect a continuance of lyric sprightliness, but must be serious often, and sometimes melancholy, else they do not express the truth of this wild world of ours; so there must be, in this magnificently human art of architecture, some equivalent expression for the trouble and wrath of life, for its sorrow and its mystery: and this it can only give by depth or diffusion of gloom, by the frown upon its front, and the shadow of its recess.

—JOHN RUSKIN,
The Seven Lamps of Architecture

The mornings had a sharp edge of chill, now, for autumn was upon the land. Bald Mountain's swamp maples were scarlet, its ash trees and its elms were golden. Among the wildflowers, only the asters and the Queen Anne's lace survived.

But very little of this, if any, Mr. Blandings saw. He was in bed. He had a cold which he was treating with a succession of strong hot toddies. He came to care less and less, in the three days of his invalidism, whether the hot toddy had any lemon or sugar in it, and eventually whether it was hot. After a succession of curious symptoms, including occasional bursts of wild, sardonic glee, he arose and resumed most of the outward appearances of his former life. But whether there could ever be any inward recovery, whether he could ever again feel the calm and euphoria he had known before he had thought to build a country sanctuary against age and want, Mr. Blandings was far from sure.

From his bed, he had heard Mr. Zucca's crew setting off its blasts; one approximately every half-hour. He had struggled against a tendency to equate every explosion against the dollars it removed from his pocketbook—dollars, it all too quickly occurred to him, he did not have. Now that his health again permitted it, he wished to have a look at things, in the hope that reality would hold fewer terrors for him if he faced it clean.

He toiled up the hill and arrived just as a blast was to be set off; he stopped abruptly, 200 yards away, warned by the foreman's shouts and arm motions. Mr. Zucca's men took up discreet positions behind trees, and the foreman himself stood at the detonating machine. He looked about him, shouted *"Fire"* in a hoarse baritone, and rammed the machine's handle downward with all the strength in his shoulders. Mr. Blandings, looking earnestly at his excavation, saw a portion of it momentarily blur as if it had gone out of focus. Then the earth shuddered, and there was a boom.

A moment later, the echoes struck back from the hills. Mr. Blandings resumed his course toward the home which, with such infinite pain, he was sculpturing out of the granite, but paused as a light patter struck the leaves of a maple above him. Four thumps and a *thwack* halted him stock-still; he had underestimated the force of the blast that was dropping fragments half the size of cobblestones in a circle about his feet. Not until all had been silent for at least a minute did Mr. Blandings venture again on his course toward the center of activity.

"When I say 'fire,' get the hell out of here," said the blasting foreman.

Mr. Blandings bridled weakly. "I'm the new owner," he said, wondering why he said it with shame instead of with pride, and then wondering why he had said it at all. It had been the attempt of a proprietor to put an artisan in his place, but it had not come off.

"Well, when I say 'fire,' get the hell out of here or you'll be the *old* owner," said the artisan. He laughed harshly. Mr. Blandings had read somewhere that men who handled dynamite and nitroglycerin suffered from headaches, occasionally very severe: apparently the foreman was having a touch of occupational migraine.

"Got any liability insurance?" asked the foreman, intent on pursuing matters to their ultimate.

"I don't know," said Mr. Blandings. It was hopeless to explain, even to himself, that in his own business he passed for a good executive. He had asked Bill Cole please to handle all the necessary policies with the real-estate man; he, Mr. Blandings, did not wish to be concerned with them. Bill Cole had told him that everything was under control, but whether liability insurance was among the heap of new policies and premium notices on his desk, Mr. Blandings truthfully did not have any idea.

"You better had have," said the foreman. "Old man from down the road was looking for you half an hour ago with fire in his eye."

"What's the matter?" asked Mr. Blandings.

"Claims a piece of rock come down on top of his prize laying hen quarter mile down the road and knocked her flatter'n a son-of-a-bitch," said the foreman. "Ask me, I think he wanted chicken for supper and figured you might as

"Old man claims a piece of rock knocked his prize laying hen flatter'n a son-of-a-bitch," said the blasting foreman.

well pay for her. He had a piece of your rock in his hand, all right, good sharp piece, but he coulda picked that up down by the mailbox. Quarter mile is a long way for this stuff to travel. Look at that lousy ledge."

Mr. Blandings looked, and could see for himself that something other than a blaster's occupational headache could well be afflicting Mr. Zucca's foreman. The rock that had once lain flat and grown thick and thicker as the epochs of lavas flowed over it, had later been heaved askew by some mountainous thrusts so that its striations now stood a bare twenty degrees from vertical. When the blasting crew set off a charge, the rock would crack and fragments would fly, but the mass would not shatter; the steam shovel's angry teeth would gnaw at it in vain. Only a crew of men with long, ten-pound crowbars could pry the broken laminations of the gneiss apart, and spread them loose for the shovel to pick up.

Mr. Blandings watched until he cared to watch no longer; then he set off slowly down the hill. Near his cottage he saw a gaunt, fierce old man in overalls who carried under his arm the plump body of a chicken whose white feathers were bespattered with blood. Apparently the old man did not recognize him as the owner whose rock blasting had cost the life of his precious hen, for he merely returned a blank, baleful glare to Mr. Blandings' tentative proffer of a good morning.

It surged over Mr. Blandings that he very much wished he were back in the city; he was uncertain whether his mind was telling him he was merely glad the final end of his vacation had almost come, or that he wanted to return to the city and stay there forever. Either way, he wanted the blessed anonymity of the city; the anonymity whereby if he saw an old man with a bloody chicken under his arm, he would merely pass by, unthinking and uncaring, free of recognition or responsibility. And he wanted the noise of the city in his ears; the noise with which all city dwellers were in such perfect, unconscious harmony that the blast of a gas main down the block might strike the eardrums, but not penetrate to the brain. The quiet of the countryside, he had learned, was merely the quiet of a capricious wrath, capriciously withheld until the supremely inopportune moment. He wanted the city's filth, too, in which only gentle, persistent, bituminous soot, not jagged rocks, fell out of the sky. He wanted privacy—and that was not to be had on a mountaintop; true privacy existed in its perfect flowering on a Bronx Park Express between five and six P.M. True detachment was to be achieved not among the rocks and rills of the countryside but on the pavements of the harsh, uncaring city, across a mile of which a man with a dagger might pursue a screaming woman with a child in her arms and evoke, in the true city dweller, no feelings other than mild wonder and philosophic speculation.

That was where he wanted to be, thought Mr. Blandings, and that, by God, was where he was going when this last week drew to its slow, tedious close. He heaved a small, tremulous sigh. He was to take the children back to school and resume his city life; his wife would stay on in the cottage and keep an eye on the construction, while he came back for week ends. It was a good arrangement; things always went better when he was not around, as his wife had already made clear to him, and it was less harrowing to be told what *had* happened than to see it in its horrid process.

EXTRACTS FROM MRS. BLANDINGS' DIARY:

October 2

Every day they say the blasting will be finished, but every day it still goes on. It's a good thing Jim is back in the city with the children. Mr. Simms and Mr. Retch and Mr. Zucca had a big fight today about how much rock had been removed so far, and Mr. Simms threatened to bring a transit over and survey the pile and prove to Mr. Zucca that it was only half what he claimed. I couldn't make out whose side Mr. Retch was on. Six trucks arrived one after another late yesterday afternoon and dumped huge piles of lumber all over the place. Mr. Simms took one look at it and says it all has to go back—checked or crazed or split or something. So am I, I guess.

October 7

I don't understand this trouble over the title to our property, which is still dragging along. A long letter from the lawyers came for Jim this morning and I opened it. They still seem to be saying they have nothing to show that Mr. Hackett was entitled to act as the Administrator of *his father's estate,* from which it seems we bought. Mr. Dolliver at the bank apparently knows all about it; he was positively *gleeful* when I bumped into him this morning, and said anybody except a dumb city bank would know that of course Ephemus was his father's Administrator and always had been ever since the old gentleman died in 1926. It would all never have come up if we had done business with him, he said. Beast! The law firm wants Mr. Hackett to post a $10,000 bond to guarantee his clearing up the final accounting and settlement of his father's estate before we get our loan, and he won't. He doesn't speak to us any more when we meet him, I don't know why. Nervous headache.

October 13

So now the blasting *is* finished—and what are we going to do with all that rock? Nobody will take any responsibility for it; even Mr. Simms just shrugged his shoulders and changed the subject when I brought it up. But there it is, a mountain of it, right where the entrance to the front door is supposed to be. I insisted that it be carried away, but Mr. Retch says there is nothing in the contract about it, and that if we want it carried away, we will have to hire a truck to do it. I read the contract twice and couldn't find a word. Maybe we could sell it to a gravel mill, or whatever they're called, if there are such things. Why is the excavation damp when we haven't had a drop of rain for over a fortnight?

October 18

Mr. Retch came down with his first "requisition" this afternoon, all signed and attested by Mr. Simms, and it was for $3765! Mr. Retch says he could use it right away, please, because he had a terrible fight with Mr. Zucca over the blasting and Mr. Zucca offered to compromise his excavation bill for a flat $1900 instead of $2341 if it was paid within a week. Jim has borrowed up to the hilt on his B & D stock to tide us over until we can get the mess with the bank's title lawyers straightened out, but I'm sure neither of us thought we would have to start laying out all these pots of money so fast before we have anything but a hole in the ground to show for it. It was nice of Mr. Retch to go to work on that Zucca man, but he keeps on talking about the money he's "saved" us, as if he had been giving it to me to put in the bank. There is something wrong with *this whole system*—I wish I knew what. In the deepest corner of the excavation there's quite a little pool of water, which I think is very odd.

October 24

There hasn't been a single solitary workman around up here for eight days now, nor the *faintest* sign of activity. Also now we're in trouble with Mr. Retch! Jim came up for the week end and said Bill Cole insisted that Mr. Retch put up a "performance bond," which I gather is something to guarantee that he'll do his work without going broke, although why anyone should worry about *him* going broke is more than I can see. Mr. Retch just sort of shrugged and Jim took that to mean O.K., but the next thing we knew Mr. Retch was down here waving a bill the bonding company had sent him for the $450 premium on the bond, and an affidavit a mile long where he's supposed to answer all sorts of questions. Mr. Retch said that if anybody was going to pay the premium, *we* were, and that the insurance company knew what it could do with its affidavit. He got quite worked up and said the chief thing that made contractors go broke was when they got mixed up with clients who didn't pay for their work, and where was the money for his requisition? But Bill Cole got a report from some credit-investigation company that Mr. Retch has gone broke three times in his life so far, and we'll be fools if we don't make him post that bond. Oh, dear, why must everything be like this? It rained a little last night, and the excavation has water in it out of all proportion, because it was just a shower.

October 29

Today the cement contractor, I guess you call him, arrived, complete with concrete mixer and all sorts of pots and pans, to start the foundation. He looked at the excavation with the water in it and said, "I should build a swimming pool?", and then he and his men just went away.

Later: Mr. Simms explained the cement contractor had gone away to get a gasoline pump, although why it took four men on a two-ton truck to get a pump, I'm sure I don't know. Mr. Simms didn't like it about there being water in the excavation, and I must say there was a lot.

November 1

The pump has been working on the excavation for two days now, and there's just as much water in it as there was when it started! Why? I didn't have much time to worry about it or anything else today. I had salesmen instead. The first one wanted to "topdress our tennis court," ha, ha. Then three tree salesmen arrived, all at the same time. I didn't know trees *had* salesmen. Finally, a little old man came along and started setting up a weather vane right in the driveway the trucks use, *and he wouldn't take it down.* He also had incinerators, estate signs, and attic ventilators for sale. I finally had to buy the weather vane to get rid of him.

November 4

Jim came up from the city just in time to hear that we have a spring in our cellar! A bubbling, bubbling spring! The cement man finally had to hitch up three pumps to get the excavation dry and when they had finally sucked all the water out, there in one corner was a place where water came *spurting* up through the rock. What I want to know is, why do men think they are so smart? They have to go down 297 feet to get water when water is what they want, but when they want something to be dry, they not only manage to find water right away but make it *spurt.* Wonderful little creatures! They don't know what they're doing three quarters of the time, but they always manage to keep on acting like the lords of creation just the same.

November 9

Who *plans* building a house? The *shingles* arrived today. Mr. Retch says what he needs is the lumber to make the forms for pouring the concrete for the foundations—and wants to know "where the hell is that?" The shingles turned out to be the wrong kind, so they had to go back, anyway. The men on the truck were pretty angry because they had them all unloaded before anybody noticed they weren't what was ordered.

November 14

So now we have a system of trenches around the foundation that looks like something on Mars and Mr. Simms says our spring is diverted, "he hopes." Now it turns out that we have to get something called a "waiver of lien" from every one of the subcontractors who are going to do work for Mr. Retch, and Mr. Retch says there'll be at least twenty of them. They all have to sign a paper promising that they won't sue us if they don't get paid for their work, and the savings bank has to have every one before we stand a chance of getting any money out of it. Some of the subcontractors obviously don't know how to write their names, so I hope it will make the bank happy to have a lot of dirty *X* marks all over their fancy papers. Why shouldn't they sue us? I bet every one of them will, anyway.

November 20

It *would* freeze in mid-November so hard the concrete man can't pour any of his stuff for the cellar walls! Jim fell in the excavation last night and hurt his knee. Glum week end.

November 25

So it unfroze, and the men started pouring the cellar walls, but Mr. Simms came along and when he saw what they were doing, he stopped the whole show, and tried to get Mr. Retch on the phone. They weren't putting more than a teaspoonful of cement into the sand and gravel, he said—a fine situation! Suppose Mr. Simms hadn't just happened to come around! Mr. Retch couldn't be reached—he was in Maryland on another job. Right after lunch a whole crew of painters arrived and when they found there wasn't any house to paint, the foreman became *abusive!* He said they had come all the way from New Jersey in answer to what he claimed was an emergency telegram Mr. Retch sent him, God knows why, saying painting must start instantly. A telephone installer arrived also, but he was very understanding and just said somebody "must have bollixed up the order sheets," and went away again.

December 1

Glory be! Bill Cole says the bank and its lawyers are almost ready for "the closing." I suppose this means we're going to get our

There wasn't any house to paint.

money at last. We're pretty far behind with all of Mr. Retch's requisitions and I certainly hope it's going to improve his disposition when this money business gets cleared up. All Jim has to do now, apparently, is give the title lawyers

$500 “in escrow” in case anything goes wrong with those beastly “waivers of lien” from those filthy subcontractors. Jim turned purple at the idea of giving Barratry, Lynch another $500, but there was nothing for him to do but write out a check just the same. Five toilets arrived today and they’re lying all around the field. They look *unspeakably* vulgar.

December 4

The woodwork is going up. I guess that’s the wrong word for it, but there are a lot of square poles sticking up in the air from the concrete foundation, and I never heard so much sawing and hammering. There must have been ten men working all around everything today. Real progress.

December 7

The name for that woodwork is “the framing.” It all got taken down again yesterday. Somebody forgot to put the copper termite pan on top of the concrete before they started putting the framing up, and Mr. Simms ordered everything into reverse. I thought he and Mr. Retch were going to come to blows.

December 10

The framing is going back up and it’s almost finished on the wing part, and I’m just sick

The toilets in the field looked unspeakably vulgar.

about *everything!* It's all *miles* too high: I thought we were getting a sweet, modest house, that hugged the hill close in its arms, and here instead is something that looks like a *grain elevator!* It just goes up and *up.* Mr. Simms was very short when I telephoned him about it, and ended up by suggesting that I "take a pill or something." He is not himself these days. I just know that *somebody* is making another *terrible* mistake. Three crates of lighting fixtures have arrived. I could scream.

December 14

Soon I will be going back to the city for the winter, thank God. I was supposed to stay here to see that things didn't go wrong, but I don't see how they could have gone wronger if I had been in Kalamazoo. But I must admit *I* was wrong about the framing being too high. Now that it's all up, it looks very nice, and *just* right. Mr. Retch was a changed man today: he got a big check to bring things almost up to date, now that we have the mortgage money after all this endless waiting. Mr. Retch says he is going to put on forced draft from here on to get everything "closed in" before the snow flies, and that the whole job is going to go "like clockwork" from here on.

December 15

Just after Jim came up for the week end, the men nailed a little tree to the top of the roof. Then they all knocked off work and came down to our cottage and stood around on one foot or another until one of them said right out that when the rooftree went up it was time for the owner to stand a round of drinks for all the workmen. Jim didn't seem to think much of this idea at first, but it's remarkable how he fell in with it after the first twenty minutes. He reached the friendly stage quite fast, and then he reached the bottoms-up stage with the boss carpenter whom he had hitherto described as "a stinking bastard." Fortunately, everybody left just before he reached the quarrelsome stage. To bed very late. Farewell, Bald Mountain. Only week ends now.

XII
Winter Week End

Another winter came to Bald Mountain, and Mr. and Mrs. Blandings saw their growing house only at irregular intervals. As he viewed it now, on a warm mid-January week end, it made Mr. Blandings think of what a flayed elephant must look like. The brick veneer which was to form the lower exterior ended at different courses in different places; above it, the diagonal sheathing of yellow pine, crusty with resin and punctured with knotholes, rose to the eaves. The roof was a wavy expanse of tar paper, dotted with the big shiny disks that acted as washers to keep the holding nails from tearing its feeble substance. The house's appearance was the nakedness of muscle, minus skin and fat.

It was being a mild January—"so far," Mr. Retch had added with truculence—and more workmen swarmed inside the house and out than Mr. Blandings would have thought necessary to fit out a destroyer. As he and his wife stood uncertainly in what appeared to be a hallway, his ear could detect half a dozen different hammers going at once, each with a pitch and frequency determined by the wood and the workman concerned with it. There was the harsh, stertorous breathing of a crosscut blade as it plowed through a soft plank; the desperate screech of a hacksaw ripping through a pipe that the hand of the workman could not keep from shuddering under the strong-set teeth. Trowels rasped on the bottom of mortarboards and then rang on brick. Unattended and malevolent, a blowtorch roared and hissed at the Blandings like a cougar's cub, its wicked flame invisible in the winter sunlight. The house smelled of hot lead, oakum, pine and redwood shavings, turpentine, sweat, linseed oil, pitch, pyroligneous acid, wet plaster, orange peels, amyl acetate, garlic, mice, a lunch somewhere forgotten, and plumbing facilities prematurely used. It all blended into something not at all unpleasant.

"Heads up!" said a voice, and Mr. and Mrs. Blandings were suddenly separated by a slab of something the size of an airplane hangar door that moved slowly past them, cradled by two workmen who stepped with the exquisite care of men handling an art treasure. They rounded a corner with elaborate caution and collided violently with a man in a derby hat and red sweater carrying a twelve-foot length of heating pipe. A shower of broken glass fragments rang musically on the planking—from where, the Blandings could not determine. No one paid the slightest attention.

"I wish you'd speak to someone about the men smoking all over the place with all this sawdust and shavings around," said Mrs. Blandings, in a nervous reaction from the broken glass. "I expect everything to go up in a puff of smoke any minute."

Mr. Blandings, in avoiding the consequences of the collision, had stepped half an inch too close to the gagging mouth of the blowtorch, and in a hypertonic reaction from this had engulfed his right hand in a can of putty. He was of no mind to answer his wife aloud, for he had just heard a voice in his inner ear respond to her injunction, with the hearty hope that everything *would* go up in a puff of smoke. He was shocked at himself. This was his home he was wishing out of existence—what was the matter with him? And why, at the very minute that he was chastising himself for such a fearful disloyalty, did the same little daemon, deeper and more maliciously than the first time, whisper to him all over again that he wished his house in hell, that he did not want it, *and never had?*

"All right, then," said a calm, methodical voice, issuing from a cavern in the wall beside the Blandings and apparently having its source in the cellar, "tell him to stick his tin snips up his ass if he don't like it." A portentous crash shook the loose planking that lay on the joists above the Blandings and served as a temporary floor; about a quarter of a pound of fine yellow powder sifted down through the wide, irregular cracks. It landed on Mr. Blandings' hat and the shoulders of his overcoat. "I want to go outside," he said.

He felt exactly as he remembered feeling once when he was three years old and was taken to his first children's party. Walking in from the friendly out-of-doors, he had suddenly encountered more crowd, heat, and noise than his infant nervous system could take; he had thrown up on the carpet, then clung to his nurse's legs and sobbed. But now he had no nurse; now he just had Mrs. Blandings, looking vexed and lumpish and unfriendly and as if to say, "Why don't you do something about it all? You're supposed to be the *man,* aren't you?"

Outside, a workman sucking a drink of water from a rubber hose looked up and said, "Howdy." He passed the back of his hand across his mouth. "Just the man I wanted to see," he said, and Mr. Blandings recognized him as Mr. Retch's oldest son and the superintendent on the job. "On them second-floor lintels between the lally columns, do you want we should rabbet them or not? From the blueprint you can't tell which way they're supposed to be."

"Well," said Mr. Blandings after a moment's pause, "well, I guess not. No, I think that's something we needn't bother with, come to think of it."

"O.K.," said Mr. Retch's son, "you're the doctor. Joe," he bawled into an inexplicable hole in the house's side, "if you got any of them rabbeted lintels set, rip 'em out. He don't want 'em that way."

There was no answer, but a moment later there was a shriek of nails brutally withdrawn from their embedment, a splintering of woods, and then, out of a second-story gape in the siding, something of the appearance of entrails came flinging end over end, to land with a dusty slap on a pile of other fragments of new, fresh-looking wood.

"Why," said Mrs. Blandings coldly, as Retch, Junior, disappeared, "did you give any definite yes or no answer to that man when you did not have the single, faintest idea what he was talking about? Now look what he's done." She scooted to the pile, examined the wreckage gingerly, and narrowly escaped a second hurtling dejection from the upper story. "Stop it," she cried to the blank opening whence it had come.

An angry man appeared in the hole, his hands on his hips. "What's biting *you?*" he inquired.

From inside the house came a long, shrill whistle. Instantly, every sound of activity ceased, and the man in the siding hole disappeared with the suddenness of a catastrophe in a Punch-and-Judy show. "O.K., fellas, let's quit," yelled a voice. The front door opened and a horde of men poured out.

What have I done? thought Mrs. Blandings, in an agony. I said something wrong; I spoke too sharply. I have precipitated a strike. She could see a small, bored headline on an inner page of a future Lansdale *Blade*: "Blandings Work Stoppage Enters Second Year."

The workmen were struggling into their overcoats now, and striding for the dozen cars parked in disorder around the Blandings manse.

"*Why* are you stopping?" asked Mrs. Blandings of a saturnine man carrying a Thermos bottle and a Stillson wrench.

"Twelve noon Saturday, lady," said the man. "Whaddaya think this is, a chain gang?"

Mrs. Blandings put her hand to her heart and breathed a little "Oh!" in sheer relief. Her moment of fear had been so acute that with its passing she felt no disposition to chide her husband further about the rabbeted mullions. She came back to the subject only after the last workman had vanished, and she and her husband were alone with their house—and then only in her mildest and most reasonable manner.

"I only thought it sounded less expensive to say no," said Mr. Blandings in a beaten voice.

The next day was Sunday, and the Blandings had the run of their house to themselves. Mr. Blandings did not like the look of the sheathing lumber, some of which had been used for the concrete forms and was still a sandy, discolored gray; he felt that he could either speak of it and make a fool of himself again or stay silent and be bilked. He chose the latter course, not as the less painful but merely as the less conspicuous. He was dismayed by the ragged lopsidedness of the holes where someday windows were supposed to be. He and Mrs. Blandings, both, were unhappy and disturbed by a remark they had heard a workman make the day before about "the damnedest, windiest site for a house I ever saw or heard of"—for indeed the wind, which always seemed mild enough elsewhere, never failed to whip and whistle around the corners of their home now that, at last, it had corners.

But the worst thing of all, the thing so bad that it produced no quarrels between the Blandings, but instead a sort of numb, wordless, animal sympathy, was the apparently microscopic size of the rooms; of the spaces, that is, where studding indicated some sort of partition arrangement in the future to be. There were five times more such spaces than even Mrs. Blandings could in any way account for, tally her closets though she might. Individually, each closet was, in her eye, totally inadequate; collectively, she admitted without duress, they consumed the house. Even the largest space of any size they could discover seemed, as the Blandings viewed it, no better than a cubicle. "Is this the *living* room?" Mrs. Blandings wailed from amidst a rectangular grove of two-by-fours. Mr. Blandings merely sat down on a nail keg and

"Is this the living room?" Mrs. Blandings wailed from amidst a rectangular grove of two-by-fours.

stared through one of the random holes in the wall, now partially covered by a heavy, filth-encrusted sheet of canvas, at a distant mountain. He no longer had the energy to appear dejected; that the plumber's blowtorch they had observed yesterday was still roaring in a closet space and no workman presumably within a dozen miles of it, called forth no notice or remark either from him or from his wife. "I *guess* it's the living room," said Mr. Blandings. "Simms warned us a room always looks this way before the partitions go up and the furniture goes in."

"Where would we have space for any furniture?" sobbed Mrs. Blandings.

"Where would we have money for any furniture?" asked Mr. Blandings.

He wandered off in an aimless way, and a moment later Mrs. Blandings heard his step on the steep ladder that gave the only access to the second floor. "Don't you go up there," said Mrs. Blandings as a creak and jar overhead indicated that Mr. Blandings was already beyond her injunction. "You'll never be able to get down."

"You can see it," said Mr. Blandings in a listless voice. "You can't see it from downstairs, but from up here you can see it plain as day. It's pink."

"What is?" asked Mrs. Blandings.

From his second-floor vantage point Mr. Blandings looked out over a view that even in the barrenness of winter had a sweep and roll and grandeur that outdid the storied Rhineland. "That hut," he said. "That damn stonemason's shack. It sticks out like a sore thumb."

Receiving no answer, he wandered away from his depressing vista and concerned himself with evidences of plumbing. Why were houses put together the way they were? he wondered. The second-floor bedrooms were outlined in only the vaguest way by vertical members here and there, and he was not walking on a floor at all but a treacherous aggregation of loose planks, yet one bathroom seemed all but finished and the others were both far advanced. All these had floors on which there was tile; and tile was partly on the walls. A toilet bowl was in place; when he looked into it he suddenly saw his wife's hat, moving about on the floor below. He made an abrupt shift in a plan that had occurred to him, and turned to the bathtub. It, too, was "positioned," as Mr. Simms would say, apparently fused at white heat into the floor and walls. The protective paper glued to its high-glaze surface was here and there torn away, and the tub was a jumble of crate slats, excelsior, shingles, bent nails, and pipe ends. It contained also a dried sandwich, a dead sparrow, and several copies of the New York *Journal-American*. A pint bottle next to the tub, with a whisky label on it and three-quarters full of a dark fluid, raised in Mr. Blandings a momentary feeling of cheer. He picked it up and sniffed it hopefully, then quickly set it down. Whatever it was, it was not what it said it was.

Below, Mrs. Blandings picked her way in her high-heeled shoes over the ruts and cracks and loose little blocks of wood that quarreled with her footing. From a convergence of piping and electrical cables, she judged that she must now be in her kitchen. It seemed long and narrow and full of darkness at noon, and two nail kegs appeared to fill it beyond its capacity, present or future. She tried to imagine some Scandinavian jewel moving about it with swift, silent efficiency and cheer, whisking a perfect dinner for eight into the candlelit loveliness of an adjoining dining room, but the picture would not come clear. She was just wondering how the swinging door of the future could possibly clear a duct overhead when she heard a distant pounding and the muffled sounds of what seemed to be her husband's voice.

"What is it now?" she asked of space.

The pounding stopped a moment and then broke out again, redoubled. "Hey!" said her husband's voice. *"Hey!"*

She retraced her steps to the foot of the ladder and called, "Where are you?"

"I'm *here,*" said Mr. Blandings' voice. "I'm stuck." His voice had a trapped sound, yet it seemed to come from out-of-doors.

"What is the matter?" said Mrs. Blandings. "Where is *here?*"

"I'm in our bathroom," said Mr. Blandings. "Come out-of-doors where you can hear me."

The statement and the command refused to coalesce in Mrs. Blandings' mind, but she did as she was bidden, and stepped through the hen-house door that marked an entrance to her home. She picked her way warily across a bright mound of curving lunes and triangles of snipped-off sheet metal, and turned her gaze upward. Her husband was at a second-floor opening in the back wall of the house, and was not at his ease.

"I'm stuck in this bloody bathroom," he said. "A gust came up and slammed the door and it's stuck shut and there isn't any hardware on it and I've busted all my fingernails trying to claw it open. Somebody's got to come up here and give it a push."

"I can't come up there," said Mrs. Blandings. "I have on high heels and I can't climb that rickety old ladder and if I could I could never get down again. I told you not to go up there in the first place."

"What do you want me to do," demanded Mr. Blandings, "stay here and starve until Monday morning?"

Husband and wife stared at one another while each tried to formulate some feasible policy of limited risk. Mr. Blandings wanted very much to get out of the bathroom, but he had no plan for bringing his wife down the ladder from the second story if, indeed, she could be persuaded to come up it in the first place. There was a long pause.

"Well, then," said Mr. Blandings, "find me a putty knife or a screw driver or something I can pry with, and tie it onto a stick and hand it up to me through the toilet bowl."

"Hand it up to you through the *what?*" asked Mrs. Blandings.

A car came bounding and scrabbling up the

Blandings' driveway-to-be. Sunday in the country was a great day for salesmen, Mrs. Blandings had learned; they could usually find a whole family trapped at once. This might be vacuum cleaners, bird baths, or still more weather vanes.

The car's engine stopped with an air of finality, and out of the front seat stepped two ladies. One was older than Mrs. Blandings; the other a few years younger. Both looked large and purposeful; discerning them, Mr. Blandings, a prisoner in his *lavabo*, shrank from the window space as though a flame-thrower had seared it.

"Hello," said the younger lady. "They told us down in the village we'd probably find you up here mooning over your castle. You got a wonderful place up here, and you got to take care of it and protect it. You got to protect your rights from a lot of crackpots and meddlers down there in Washington that's getting all set to fix it so's people can't build their own house and enjoy their rights to it without getting some college professor's say-so. That's what the Republican Party in this state is bound and determined to put a stop to and that's why Mrs. Ortig and me are here right now to get a contribution for the State Committee from anybody's got the brains and money to build a beautiful home right here on top of this mountain that they got to protect if they want to save their God-given right to enjoy it."

"My husband is stuck in the bathroom," said

Mrs. Blandings, whose mind changed subjects slowly under certain conditions.

The ladies turned a hearty gaze on the shrinking object in the hole in the siding, who had never had less stomach for politics than now. "Why, blessums little heart," said the younger one. "Why don't you go get him out? He looks real nice."

Mr. Blandings wondered why it was always at the hands of women that he received life's blackest and deepest humiliations. His position as a hostage to the Republican State Committee swept over him with a clarity akin to nausea. "Jump," said the younger one. "Momma'll catch you."

Mr. Blandings' attempts to live up to the occasion were so piteous that in a moment the younger woman changed her tack; she strode into the house and despite her size scurried up the ladder with the agility of a squirrel. A thump of her palm swung the bathroom door ajar, and Mr. Blandings walked out into Freedom—Freedom save for a moral commitment to the Republican State Committee that needed no emphasis in any of the four minds that contemplated it.

"Thanks," said the younger apostle of right-thinking as she snapped her purse shut on the pledge card to which Mr. Blandings had signed his name, after writing the word "fifty" on a dotted line in front of the printed word "dollars." "If you ever get stuck in that nasty old johnny again, just yell for Isabella Rorty and I'll come a-running. Come on, Madge. Maybe Joe Klemper down the road has fell through his privy and we'll get another fifty bucks out of him."

They departed in a breeze of good humor, leaving the newly enrolled member of the Republican Party to wonder what he should have done instead of what he had done. He could not seem to come to a conclusion. His speedy conquest by Isabella Rorty made him, he imagined, the only enrolled Republican in the party's history who had voted for Franklin Delano Roosevelt on every occasion so far possible in his political life; he wondered what the Rorty woman would have done with his check had he had the courage to tell her. In the city, he had never needed to make a secret of his political views, even in his rare discussions with Mr. Banton or Mr. Dascomb, heavyweight Republicans both. But the countryside had defeated him again—in its hands he was now a hypocrite as well as a despoiler. Hereafter, in Lansdale County, if he were still to hold his convictions, he would somehow or other have to belong to the Democratic Underground. Perhaps he would *be* the Democratic Underground; in his year and a half of Lansdale community acquaintanceship he had yet to encounter a Roosevelt collaborationist, however mild.

Mr. Blandings remained in an outward aspect of quiet dignity for the balance of the week end, but although he seemed in a mood clay-soft to the suggestions of others, Mrs. Blandings felt it would be a mistake to test her luck too far.

XIII
The Wind in the Windows

"We enclose," said the letter, "our check for the final payment on the amount of $18,000 which we have been happy to advance to you, secured by a First Mortgage on your property on Bald Mountain."

It was the mortgage officer of the Seagate-Proletarian Savings Bank who was addressing Mr. Blandings on his institution's crackliest engraved stationery.

"Our building inspection committee had the pleasure of visiting your site earlier this week, and I take this opportunity of passing on to you some of the extremely enthusiastic comments I heard expressed. One of our members, particularly familiar with this area, said that he knew of no site more impressive in any other part of our state, which is saying a great deal, and all joined in admiration of your and your architect's plans. You are building a fine house on a location with the most genuinely strategic advantages and the bank is pleased to have a part in so constructive an investment.

"New builders are occasionally discouraged by the complications and unforeseen circumstances with which the construction industry sometimes confronts them, but things have a curious habit of turning out all right in the end, and I hope you and Mrs. Blandings will live for many years to enjoy the fruits of your industry and imagination."

It just couldn't have been a nicer letter, the Blandings agreed. And it couldn't be anything but sincere. Mr. Blandings had the bank's money, the bank had his note, and obviously nothing was being served by such a communication except spontaneous and sincere good will. "By God, we're going to come out of this all right," said Mr. Blandings, and took down from a shelf the set of Mr. Simms's original drawings he had not looked at for a long time. Mrs. Blandings was happy to see that within a minute he was completely absorbed.

There was nothing so, well, so *aphrodisiac,* as a set of building plans, Mr. Blandings said to himself. Even in the days when the Blandings' idea of a new home was merely a different apartment out of which someone else had just moved, the plans, with their thick black lines and their crisp lettering, had roused in them an instinct that obviously was something deeper and finer than mere cupidity. It was the nest-building instinct, damn it, thought Mr. Blandings, and let anybody go ahead and laugh who wants to. His head buried in Mr. Simms's exquisite draftsmanship, Mr. Blandings was dreaming again; dreaming happily. The vexations and

There was nothing so, well, so aphrodisiac, as a set of building plans.

frustrations and checks and naggings of mischance were all in the proper perspective of the far and insignificant background; something for a hearty laugh in the days when the Blandings' house would be a mellowed, weathered shrine; ivy-shrouded, garlanded with lilac, the shade trees casting their waving silhouettes upon the pure green suede of an English lawn.

The next week-end visit to Bald Mountain sustained the owners' recaptured calm. It had snowed hard earlier in the week, and now it was clear and cold. It took Mr. Blandings a tussle with car chains to get his station wagon urged up the reverse-curve slopes of Bald Mountain, but it was worth every ounce of steamy breath, every drop of the freezing sweat, it cost. The dry snow blew like smoke across the fields and roadways; around every tree trunk was a circle of flashing bits of ice. At the site, the incredible, undifferentiated rubbish of lumber ends, cracked pipe sections, bits of tin and scraps of wire that were the castoffs of construction were all buried under gentle swells and folds of snow.

The house was quiet. The house was far too quiet. Where a dozen workmen had been scurrying like ferrets the week before, today there was not a soul to be seen, and the house appeared to have made the least possible progress consistent with not vanishing.

A faint jangle from the cellar indicated some form of activity, and Mr. Blandings clumped down the rough steps to search it out. Sitting cross-legged on a plank flung across the icy concrete floor was a young man with his back to Mr. Blandings. He was surrounded by a welter of tubes and sheets of thin metal, and as he flourished a pair of heavy tin snips in his right hand, he whistled a toneless tune. Apparently he had heard no visitor approach.

"Morning," said Mr. Blandings. The young man turned about, and Mr. Blandings was confronted with the stonemason from down the road whose shack was so deep a source of distress to him.

"Howdy," said the young man. "Wondered when I'd be bumping into you again. How's things with you and the Hysterical Society? All blowed over like I told you, I guess."

"Yes," said Mr. Blandings, feeling embarrassed and not knowing precisely why. "All blown—all blowed over, so far as I can see, just like you said."

"Some people seem to like to spend all their time sticking their nose into other people's business," said the young man. "Now you take me, I wouldn't care what you're up to, so long as you leave me go *my* way, like I leave you go yours."

"That's right," said Mr. Blandings.

"You take some of the workmen around here," said the young man. "They got themselves all lathered up about you. They—"

"About *me?*" said Mr. Blandings.

"Sure," said the young man. "They go round muttering what's this Blandings guy think he's up to, building an ark up here top this mountain that's been Hackett's mountain ever since God was a small boy. I tell 'em this is a free country, ain't it? I don't know who this Blandings is, I tell 'em, but if he's got money to pay me a day's wages, I'll give him a day's work and not ask any questions."

"I thought you were a stonemason," said Mr. Blandings.

"I work at that summers," said the young man. "That and raising a garden. Winters I cut these paper dolls out of sheet metal for Woskowski."

Mr. Blandings recognized the name of the plumbing-and-heating subcontractor. The young man picked up a sheet of galvanized metal; it shivered and sighed like a cymbal lightly struck. He held an edge of it up to a junction of two air-heating ducts, one an elliptical cylinder, one a truncated cone. He squinted along its edge, and made two marks with a heavy pencil. Then he cut into it with bold authority, and Mr. Blandings saw curling off from it a spiral that Archimedes had never dreamed of.

"I studied that in college once," said Mr. Blandings. The young man's easy, cheerful competence made him think of his vanished friend, John Tesander.

"Tinsmithing? In college?" said the young man. "You're kiddin'."

"No," said Mr. Blandings; "I mean descriptive geometry."

"I wouldn't know about that," said the young man. "I quit high school after the first year. All right for some folks, but not my dish."

Mr. Blandings remembered the brain-racking, hand-palsying torture of the college course in descriptive geometry he had struggled through in his freshman year. It was half mathematics and half draftsmanship, and it was concerned to systematize the way that planes and solids intersect other planes and solids, and what quasi-mathematical laws the boundaries of such sections might obey. Mr. Blandings had struggled mightily for months and achieved a barely passing grade; now he watched while this young man, working in a temperature that had Mr. Blandings' fingers stiff with cold, did by instinct with obstinate metal what the whole vast educational force of Yale University had found it all but impossible to teach Mr. Blandings to do on pliant, yielding paper. Into what outline should one edge of metal sheeting be cut so that when the sheet was wrapped into a cylinder it would form a cuff fitting at every point with the indescribable curve of its fellows? As Mr. Blandings watched the young man walk his tin snips through the metal, a sculptor of edges and hollows, it was no trick at all. By what queer sort of accident, plus what queer sort of complacence, was this chap a journeyman plumber instead of a young sculptor or a surgeon, Mr. Blandings wondered.

"Where's everybody else today?" he asked.

"Too cold for 'em, I guess," said the young man. "But it ain't going to get any warmer in here until I get these ducts so that we can set the furnace. You could do with some windows in your house, too."

"I sure could," said Mr. Blandings. "I guess everybody doesn't like to work as much as you do. Maybe that's because they're not as good workmen."

The young man rode roughshod and unheeding over the compliment.

"Listen," he said. "You got some very good mechanics on this job of yours."

I must remember, thought Mr. Blandings, that in this part of the country you don't call a workman a workman unless he's a ditchdigger; if he's skilled, you call him a mechanic, whether he's a carpenter or a mason or a plumber.

"You got some fairly lousy ones, too," the young man went on. "It ain't up to me to tell you which is which, but you could see for yourself if you'd take a look. I kid 'em, when I see 'em cutting corners on you. I tell 'em, listen, the owner's human too, you know, even if he is a millionaire, so don't screw the poor bastard *every* time he turns around, I tell 'em; just every other time."

"I appreciate that," said Mr. Blandings. He meant it. He had a slight taste of wormwood in him from the venomous mistrust he had held for this young man as a neighbor half a mile away. "Maybe," he said, in a compensating burst of friendliness, "maybe when we've got the house finished you and your wife will come up to see us. You only live half a mile away."

"Sure we'll be up," said the young man. "My wife'll probably bring your wife some seedlings to get her garden started with, or something. If I was you I'd beat it now before you freeze. You ain't used to this."

"Well," said Mr. Blandings, warm with friendship, "so long, then." He started up the stairs, and paused on the third step. "I guess I don't know your name," he said.

"Hackett," said the young man. "Old Eph is one of my uncles. Don't never trust him further than you can throw a grand piano. Him and that Mrs. Prutty is cousins, and old Anson Dolliver you tangled with down to the bank, he's her son-in-law. Just o-n-e b-i-g family you got mixed up with. Someday I'll give you the password."

I am making progress, Mr. Blandings thought. Someday I will really know the ins and outs of this community, after all. A few more happy encounters like that, and I will be able to get around without a sheep dog. But first I must get my house finished, and to do that I must have some windows, as the young Hackett chap so succinctly pointed out.

First thing Monday morning in the city, he phoned Mr. Retch.

By some miracle Mr. Retch was in his office, and not supervising a job in Vermont. Ordinarily callous to a client's appeals for progress, Mr. Retch turned out to be in a state of sympathetic irritation about the windows, and assured Mr. Blandings he wanted them worse than anybody else. How could he build a house and collect the money he sorely needed without a little co-operation from suppliers?

The next thing Mr. Blandings knew he was so mixed up with his windows that there seemed little room in his life for anything else; care once again perched on his shoulder and resumed its pecking at his breast. A window-casement company was a new experience in his life—an experience he felt he was having both too early and too late.

The window truck had left the factory and would be on the site tomorrow. No, the truck had not left; there was no truck. The windows had been shipped by freight as all windows are the world over; if they had not arrived, the freight car must have been put on a wrong siding by a demented brakeman. No, the windows would be shipped by truck *when* they were ready; this would not be for another five weeks. No, the windows could be nowhere but on the site, and must have been mislaid by the contractor. No, an order for the windows had never been received, but "we would give your valued custom promptest attention should we be so favored."

When, in a surprisingly short time, a great load of windows arrived by truck, Mr. Blandings experienced a supreme but impermanent pleasure. They were for a house apparently being built by a man named Landers in Fishkill, New York, and had no other congruence with the lives of Mr. and Mrs. Blandings. A long-distance telephone call to Mr. Landers to see if the two shipments had been confused revealed that Mr. Landers had just received a huge consignment of windows addressed to "Blankenthorn Job, Pueblo, Colorado," and was himself suffering from vexation; he deeply resented any suspicions that he had Mr. Blandings' windows, he wanted his own windows, he wanted them quick, and as God was his witness, he was going to get them if he had to pry them out of Mr. Blandings with a pinch bar.

Mr. Blandings felt a strong sense of triumph when, after a while, roughly half his own windows actually arrived and the truckmen dumped them in a disorderly pile in the roadway. Four of them looked like velocipedes that had been run over by the Lake Shore Limited, but at least they were now on the site.

Several days later two window installers arrived, very drunk; they looked at the windows and roamed away, to return at their pleasure.

Mr. Blandings, some weeks later, ventured to inquire of Mr. Retch why some work could not go forward, even in the absence of the remaining windows or any crew to install them. This inquiry struck Mr. Retch as in the most flagrant bad taste. The windows had from the outset, Mr. Blandings now discovered, been a matter of discord between

Mr. Retch, who hated the window company's guts, and Mr. Simms, who considered it the Tiffany of the trade. Mr. Simms had written it into the contract that the windows were to be installed by the window company's own artisans, not by Mr. Retch's crew—"and you saw them two drunken goats that's supposed to be the only kind of mechanics with enough know-how to touch the Christ-bitten things." It further developed that the window company had not been persuaded into signing Mr. Blandings' waiver of lien until Mr. Retch paid spot cash in advance for every one—the window company having been a sufferer from a financial embarrassment in Mr. Retch's earlier professional life, as Mr. Simms confided to Mr. Blandings at one particular deep stage of general conspiratorial confusion.

Now that the window company had Mr. Retch's money, it was letting him whistle for his windows out of sheer commercial malevolence, Mr. Retch explained. In coarse tones he outlined to Mr. Blandings that *(a)* the mason subcontractor was stalled in his tracks since he could not complete his brick courses around the missing frames; *(b)* no finished siding could even begin to be nailed to the sheathing; *(c)* not even the subfloors could be properly laid when the house was still open to rain and snow; *(d)* it was manifest now that the plastering could never be started until spring, if then; *(e)* tile courses in the bathrooms were stalled just as the brickwork was stalled; *(f)* the electrical subcontractor refused to run any more BX cable around wet joists and columns; *(g)* the heating subcontractor could make no further progress until the house was closed in. Finally, *(h)* until blockade *g* was lifted no more workmen were likely to show up until spring, anyway. He ended by predicting that if he did coerce a crew into doing some odds and ends, they would probably burn the house down with one or another of the informal fires they had already found it necessary to build to keep them sufficiently warm to drive a tack. On whose shoulders would this responsibility then rest? Mr. Retch inquired.

Suddenly enough windows arrived to build a biscuit factory.

Out of an infinite variety of rectangular steel shapes Mr. Retch selected those frames which seemed to accord roughly with the dimensions on Mr. Simms's plans, and sought to get the window company to send back a crew of window installers, preferably sober enough to put the windows into the sheathing holes right side up.

Some days later the same two window installers returned, bearing with them the tools of their skilled profession, which turned out to be hatchets. They now had the bland appearance and happy demeanor of men at the beginning of a drunk, rather than the harassed patterns, such as they had displayed before, that characterize a conclusion. They hacked away with cheerful abandon at the two-by-fours in the vicinity of the roughed window openings, and into these enlarged and irregular holes they began jamming the delicate steel frames. The local workmen of Mr. Retch's own crew looked on with dour suspicion as these $12-a-day specialists went about their exacting tasks, but elaborately kept out of their way. Mr. Retch implied to Mr. Blandings that there would have to be some extra charges on his own next requisition for general repairs to the house framing and sheathing in the vicinity of the windows as soon as the installers (whom he now referred to with exquisite politeness as "the Swiss watchmakers") had completed their close-tolerance work.

After about a week the installers announced that the condition of their health would make their further attendance upon Mr. Blandings' project impossible. A recurrent arthritis was bothering the senior one, he explained; the other, an asthma sufferer since birth, had been most adversely affected by the altitude; other arrangements would have to be made. They departed in the early afternoon, staggering slightly from their disabilities and with clear suggestions to Mr. Blandings that they were going to sue him for permitting penal working conditions on his job as expressly prohibited by several clauses in the State Workmen's Compensation Act which they cited extensively. They left behind them eight window frames still uninstalled in random locations, and a set of steel doors to the Blandings' sun porch affixed at the bottoms but not the tops.

It was at about this time that Mrs. Blandings discovered all the bathtubs in the house to be deeply and disfiguringly scratched.

Not even Mr. Retch and the plumbing subcontractor, when Mrs. Blandings faced them, could deny or depreciate the facts. Most of the rubbish in the tubs had been thrown out the windows, but the heavy protective paper glued to the tubs' interiors had not been enough to keep a profusion of glacial grooves from the dense porcelain surfaces. Nor did it take any heavy inductive process to determine how the scratches had got there: the windows in all four bathrooms were directly over the tubs; anyone working at the windows would have had to stand in the tubs, but need not have stood in them with hobnail boots, and without a square of old carpet to protect them. The local workmen of Mr. Retch's crew had all seen the installers standing on the porcelain, they now eagerly averred, but it had not occurred to them to mention it or offer remonstrance at the time. The plumbing subcontractor, until now a quiet and orderly Pole, fell into a passionate torrent of abuse directed at Mr. Retch, and vowed that any attempt to fix the responsibility for the

The plumbing contractor fell into a passionate torrent of abuse.

tub damage on *him* would only result in deep misfortune for all. Mr. Retch allowed that *somebody* was going to have to replace the tubs but that by God it wasn't going to be him; he would, that is to say, happily replace the tubs at a per diem rate when new ones were obtained, but who was going to pay for the new ones—which would cost some $75 each? The plumbing subcontractor declaimed that this was just what he had suspected: the beginnings of a conspiracy to fasten onto his guiltless shoulders the onus that the architect would now obviously not certify the tubs as satisfactory, or entitle him to collect on his contract for honest work, honestly done. Since the plumbing subcontractor was also the heating subcontractor, he immediately ordered a cessation of all his work on the premises until adjudications should be satisfactorily completed, and the faint current of warmed air which had begun at last to circulate through the partially closed-in Blandings Job immediately ceased. Conditions then reverted to approximately what they had been a month or more before, except that the Blandings now had some of their windows more or less installed, but had traded this advantage for the necessity of having four 500-pound bathtubs ripped out of the tiled walls and floors into which they had for some weeks been securely affixed, and new ones installed, subject to some future delivery. It remained to be seen who would pay for what. Mr. Retch brimmed over Mr. Blandings' cup of hemlock by pointing out that the house was now at such a stage that there were no remaining openings large enough to admit new bathtubs except the bathroom window openings themselves. The tubs would have to be hoisted up to them—and, of course, the frames removed. By whom? Mr. Retch asked.

Mr. Retch faced the window company with the responsibility for its vagrant workmen. Just what Mr. Retch said to the window company over the telephone, Mr. Blandings did not know, but with lightning speed the window company called Mr. Blandings direct to say that his contractor had been grossly abusive over the telephone on the general subject of bathtubs, which was obviously no concern of theirs since they were manufacturers and installers of window frames which were in no way connected with the bathtub industry, as any fool should know; that even if bathtubs *were* their concern, they would still resent having been treated by this chiseling contractor with an illiterate insolence never previously known within their experience of fifty years in making and selling the best windows in the building trade; that finally and furthermore they would within the next three days send a special crew from their headquarters to remove from the house *and* from the site every window that bore their trade-mark, since the check for $1407.56 with which Mr. Retch had paid for the windows had been returned to them marked "insufficient funds." When Mr. Blandings relayed this intelligence to Mr. Retch, Mr. Retch went rooting in a vast pile of papers and produced a check to the order of the window company for the precise figure under discussion, stamped and canceled by the bank as paid. He added that in thirty years in the construction industry this was the first time an owner had ever accused him of fraud, and that if Mr. Blandings would like to, they could settle the affair outside; if Mr. Retch lost, he would build the rest of Mr. Blandings' house at his own expense.

It was at this date that Mrs. Blandings discontinued her diary with the notation that she was taking the children to Sarasota for the balance of the winter and installing them in an outdoor school for the benefit of their sinuses. She did not mention the house at all. Of Mr. Blandings she merely recorded that he was "better."

XIV
Extras

LETTER TO MR. JOHN RETCH FROM J. H. BLANDINGS:

March 2

It is some time since my wife or I have visited the house and my hope is that the work is progressing as fast as the receipt of money requisitions from you would seem to indicate. We will hope to get up again as soon as the weather moderates.

Meanwhile, I am considerably disturbed by the number of "extras" that are accumulating on your bills. So far as my wife and I are aware, we have authorized only two changes from the original plans as O.K.'d. For one, the depth of the reveal at the front door was altered by Mr. Simms with our approval after the framing was complete. For another, we also authorized the relocation and redesign of the outdoor concrete cellar steps after Mrs. Blandings fell down them. Except for these items, which seem to total $677.60, God knows why, I am at a loss to understand the multitudes of other matters being billed me, or, in some cases, what the items specified

Mr. Blandings was considerably disturbed by the number of extras.

refer to at all. I herewith quote and comment on the following from your latest requisitions:

"*Redesign of doorways No. 102, 107, 108, 112* $220.00"
(Mr. Simms assures me that there was no redesign on any doorways on the job whatsoever.)

"*New Installation of well casing* $96.50"
(If, according to your own explanation, the well casing installed by Mr. John Tesander on

his separate and previous contract with me was cracked by the blasting done by your excavation subcontractor, I fail to see why I should bear the cost of the replacement.)

"*Substitution of 220-volt switch panel in cellar* $139.89"

(What is the meaning of this? It seems to be one of a series of innumerable extras on the electrical work. When we discussed the original bid of the electrical subcontractor, you told me with what I took at the time to be frankness that he was a good man "but liked to bid low and add extras." *You suggested that I should add $500 to his contract figure before he started work* because "that'll please him and you'll save in the long run." I would like to know what I have saved by what turns out to be a charitable contribution, since I cannot imagine getting more extras than I have had, anyway. As to this switch panel, why has something been substituted for something else without my knowledge until it comes time to pay for it?)

"*Furring down ceiling for kitchen cabinets* $102.00"

(Insofar as I understand this charge, I consider it outrageous. You have known the dimensions of the kitchen cabinets from the beginning; if you did not, then you were guilty of negligence. And yet you have the effrontery to put this on my bill as an extra!)

“*Mortising five butts* $1.68”

(This refers to something I do not understand, and the charge is small—but apparently when you can think of a way of billing me for a carpenter picking up an extra chisel, you do so. Also, are your cost-accounting methods really so accurate that you know this should cost me $1.68 instead of $1.66 or even $1.71?)

“*Furnishing and installing one*
Zuz-Zuz Water Soft-N-R $265.50”

(I will not have any such piece of equipment in my house. Who authorized it? So far as I am concerned it can be taken out immediately—nor will I pay any subsequent extra labeled “Removal of Zuz-Zuz Water Soft-N-R.”)

“*Extra Screws* $3.00”

(A very modest sum, but wouldn’t it be more customary for you to pay me?)

All this totals $828.57—a not inconsiderable sum. I will expect to hear from you directly and to have these evident misunderstandings cleared up without cost to me. Also, I wish you would ask your bookkeeper to stop writing “Please!” in red ink across the bottom of these bills. I am cleaning up your legitimate charges as quickly as I find it possible.

EXTRACT FROM LETTER TO MR. J. H. BLANDINGS FROM JOHN RETCH:

. . . only time in our experience when an owner has taken any such position. We have passed up many extra items without bill, because we wanted you to be satisfied all along the line. Pardon our suggestion that you and Mrs. Blandings ought to get together, but furring down of kitchen ceiling was discussed with her, and she told us kitchen cabinets had to fit exactly “at all costs.” We could have installed lighter electrical switch panel against advice of electrical contractor, who is more of a specialist in such things than any architect, no matter how good, and leave resulting fire hazard up to you, but preferred to take the honest course of making the equipment adequate to the heavy electrical load your lines will be carrying and bill you in the open, after calling architect’s attention to same. The Zuz-Zuz people make a fine water softener and you will not regret having the benefit of this equipment. We put it in because we were looking out for your interests in not letting your boilers and water lines be ruined by the water from your well which the plumbing man assured us was the most corrosive water in his entire experience in the trade. We discussed this with Mr. Simms when we could not get ahold of you and he said he would explain these circumstances, which it appears he did not. As to the well casing . . .

TO MR. JOHN RETCH FROM J. H. BLANDINGS:

. . . and I enclose a check for $828.57, but will positively not be responsible for any further . . .

"We'll raise a fund of two billion dollars," said Mr. Simms in a tired voice. "I'll contribute to it myself—as generously as I can. So will every other architect in the country. We'll use it so that every man, woman, or child who wants to build a house can build a practice one, free of charge. As soon as it's built, it gets torn down, and *then* if the state gives you a certificate of competency, you can build a house for keeps at your own expense. Two billion dollars is a lot of money, but I think the economy of the U.S. would suffer less that way than this."

"That is very amusing," said Mr. Blandings, who had developed a twitch in his right eyelid. "But what I'm trying to talk about is this latest, final, outrageous piece of larceny from your colleague, Mr. Retch."

". . . and I enclose a check for $828.57 but will positively not be responsible for any further . . ."

He waved the paper he was holding in his tremulous hand. It was a special bill from Mr. Retch; as Mr. Blandings looked at it for the tenth time, he felt the same tendency to scream and smash that had swept him when he first unfolded it. On the bill was typed only one line:

Changes in closet $1247.00

"I would venture to say," said Mr. Blandings, "there is no closet in the Taj Mahal that ever cost

$1247 to construct *new,* to say nothing of merely *changing* it. We have a hell of a lot of closets in this house, I am the first to admit, but if Mr. Retch decided we needed to have one enlarged to keep a burlap bagful of emeralds in, he decided without consulting me."

"On my copy there's a notation that says it refers to changes on Detail Sheet No. 135," said Mr. Simms. "That's in the back of the house someplace—around the back pantry, unless I'm mixed up. Let me find that sheet."

Mr. Simms rose and made for the table on which his great volume of blueprints lay curly and dog-eared. Mrs. Blandings, who had been sitting quietly sewing in a corner, arose as he did. Making for the sideboard, she poured herself a generous slug of whisky, downed it at a gulp, and resumed her seat. Her husband watched her with amazement. Mrs. Blandings usually drank with reluctance and only when her duties as a hostess made her think it the part of graciousness. I guess she has a cramp, thought Mr. Blandings; she has that sort of drawn look she gets.

"Well, it really isn't a closet at all," said Mr. Simms; "it's that recess with the flower sink off the back entryway. We designed it while we were working on the closets, and I guess it's always stayed that way on Retch's charts. But God knows why there'd be any changes there."

Mr. Blandings continued to glare at him, the

baleful effect he was seeking somewhat marred by his twitching eyelid. Mrs. Blandings, returned to her sewing, was mouselike in the corner, but a flush had gained her cheek.

"Wait a minute," said Mr. Simms, looking up from his blueprints. "There was a bluestone floor in there when I looked at it the other day, and I said to myself I must be slipping; I could have sworn we just had a continuation of the pantry floor in there. Then I thought maybe we'd decided to bring the flag floor in there from the breezeway instead. But right here on my detail, it shows a wood floor, just as I thought."

Mr. Blandings, who could be extremely slow to achieve the sum of two and two when on the defensive, could also be as swift as a striking cobra when his own conscience was clear. His wife's silence, her flush, the incredible gulp of whisky, and the flower sink, a pet and favorite project from the day she had first thought of it, arranged themselves suddenly in his mind. He did not know what he had, but he knew he had something. He pivoted slowly from the waist and faced his wife. He had been the prisoner in the dock for a year; suddenly he had become the guardian of Justice—black-robed, bewigged, and awesome.

"What—have—you—done?" he demanded.

"I never heard of anything so ridiculous," said Mrs. Blandings. "I haven't done a thing, and what

"What—have—you—done?" demanded Mr. Blandings.

I did has nothing to do with what we're talking about and I don't see why I should be bullied about my flower sink."

It was said too fast, and it did not hang together. Even Mr. Simms, who infinitely preferred Mrs. Blandings' fussy exactitudes to Mr. Blandings' vague expansivenesses, began to look stern.

"All I did," said Mrs. Blandings, "all I did was one day I saw four big pieces of flagstone left over from the porch that were just going to be thrown away because nobody wanted them and I asked Mr. Retch if he wouldn't just put them down on the flower of the floor sink—you're getting me all rattled—the floor of the flower sink and poke a little cement between the cracks and give me a nice stone floor where it might be wet with flowers and things. That was absolutely every bit of all I did."

Mr. Simms put his head in his hands and closed his eyes. Mrs. Blandings, who only expected to be told that she had done something mildly wrong for which she would receive a gentle chastisement, stared at the silent suffering of her architect with a wild feeling of alarm. Mr. Blandings looked from his wife to Mr. Simms and back again, and a thick, towering silence grew and grew. After a while Mr. Simms took his hands down from his face and shook his head as if to clear his ears.

"Well," he said, "I'll go to Retch and see if I can't argue a hundred dollars off his extra someplace or other. It *is* a little steep."

"But good God!" said Mr. Blandings. "That would still leave over a thousand dollars for setting four lousy pieces of flagstone down around a sink. I don't—"

"Come to think of it, I saw a drain in that floor," said Mr. Simms. "The stone is sloped to drain in the middle and there's a little catch basin cemented into the flags. I guess I won't be able to get a hundred dollars off, but I'll certainly try for seventy-five.

Tell me *just* what you said to Mr. Retch, Mrs. Blandings. Did you authorize a drain, too?"

"Of course I didn't," said Mrs. Blandings, tears almost but not quite coming to rescue her from male persecution. "All I said was that what I wanted was a nice stone floor put down so that I could splash around with my flowers if I wanted to. And Mr. Retch was as nice as could be, and said, 'You're the doctor,' and that's all anybody ever said to anybody about anything."

"All right," said Mr. Simms. He seemed better, now the uncertainty was over. "I think I can tell you everything that happened, just as if I'd seen it all myself. First, the carpenters had to rip up the floorboards that were already laid. Those planks run under the whole width of the pantry, so Retch had to knock the bottom out of the pantry wall to get them out. Then he had to saw them off. Then he had to relay them in the pantry. Then he would have had to chop out the tops of the joists under the flower-sink space to make room for a cradle. He could have built a cradle out of wood, but he 'likes to do things right,' as he's fond of saying, so I guess he bought some iron straps and fastened them to a big pan to give him something to hold the cement he was going to lay those flagstones up in. What with that added load on the weakened joists, I'll bet he had to put a lally column down there for support, too. Do you mind if I have a drink?"

In the absence of any response from his hosts, Mr. Simms mixed himself a highball and resumed his chair. Vistas were opening up in his mind with startling and exact clarity.

"Well," he said, "the main soil pipe runs right under there on wall brackets in the cellar, so Retch had to get his plumbing man back to take out a section of it so he could get that cradle set. I guess that meant he had to change the pitch of the soil pipe from one end of the house to the other; you can't just put a sag in it, you understand, unless you want the sewage to run backwards, which I sometimes think would be a good idea, but which is currently prohibited by law. So he had to change his connections at the far end of the house, too, to take care of the new pitch. And then, of course, he had to throw one pipe section out and put in another one with a *Y* in it, so he could hitch on for that drain he was fixing up for you. Lucky he had such a short run. There are hot and cold water pipes hooked to the joists right under there, too, going up to the wing bathroom on the second floor, so I'll bet my bottom dollar he had to relocate *them.* And I guess the electrician had to rip out about sixty feet of armored cable between the main panel and the junction box by the oil burner, including the 220-volt cable that goes to the stove. Oh, yes, and there was a heating duct in the way, too. I'll bet that duct took somebody three days to finagle with, all by itself."

Mr. Simms took a long pull on his glass. "So then he put his cradle in, and then he called back his mason contractor and got him to work that stone, including the work around the catch basin, which was a nice dainty-looking job, as I saw it. But he couldn't get the whole thing quite as low as he would have liked to because there was a limit to how much his plumber could lower his soil line, and *that*"—Mr. Simms was obviously forgetting the somberness of his subject in his pleasure at reconstructing all this from a one-line bill—"and that's why the back door was off last time I was up there. There'd be three doors that wouldn't clear the floor any more because he would have had to raise his level, but two of them were closet doors, so I guess he'd figured he could deal with them himself. But that heavy back door leading onto the breezeway, I guess he thought he'd better send that one back to the mill, just to be safe."

He paused, and still there was no sound from Mr. or Mrs. Blandings.

"I guess that was about the size of it," said Mr. Simms. "Except then Retch had to repair the pantry wall and that meant getting a plasterer back, and the wire-lath man, too. And—for goodness sake, I forgot all about it—Retch couldn't even have got at that pantry wall to break through it until he'd taken down that built-in sink closet, taken the sink off, and disconnected its pipes back down to the cellar. Quite an undertaking. Let's see—carpenters, plumber, electrician, plasterer, lather, mason, tinsmith for the heating ducts, a couple of floor-layers (they're not the same as ordinary carpenters, you know)—it took all those people on the site, plus a blacksmith and a frame-and-sash millworker in their own shops, to get those four flagstones laid down in that little recess. If I can't get Retch to knock $75 off his extra, I'll certainly sweat $50 out of him."

"Does—" said Mrs. Blandings.

"Be quiet," said Mr. Blandings.

"Now look," said Mr. Simms. "The trouble with virgin builders like you people isn't merely that you short-circuit me and give orders for the house *I'm* trying to build for you, that either confuse or duplicate or merely bitch up the orders I'm trying to give—it's that you don't even know when you're saying good morning to the contractor and when you're authorizing him to spend over a thousand dollars of your money. If you weren't to pay Retch's bill for this, and if he were to sue you for it, and you were to tell in court what you've just told me, the judge would instruct the jury to find for Retch and if they didn't, he'd throw their verdict out of court."

"Does—" said Mrs. Blandings.

"Be quiet," said Mr. Blandings. "I wouldn't mind about women so much if it wasn't that they wanted to *chatter* all the time."

"The trouble with an owner on his site," said Mr.

Simms, "is that he or his wife thinks that asking the contractor to do something they've just thought of is like asking the cook to put another potato in the saucepan now that she's got the water boiling. But it isn't like that. It isn't like that at all. The difference between that and asking a contractor to put down four little squares of flagstone when a house is three-quarters finished is just about"—he glanced at Mr. Retch's fluttering slip of paper—"just about $1247. When you build your next house, you'll know that."

"If—" said Mrs. Blandings, but stopped there at a look from her husband.

"Well," said Mr. Simms, "I've got to be going. It's a lot later than I thought. I guess Retch saw a fairly good thing in this, and a chance to make up some money he might have lost someplace else on the job and kept his mouth shut about. I guess he thought to himself, If this is what the owner's wife is asking for, this is what she's going to get. He should have warned you, but I guess he must have been feeling pretty tired. At that, there's nothing that's not legitimate. You gave him a chance, and he took it."

He paused at the door. "Of course," he said, "my ten per cent fee doesn't get added for little items like this. I wouldn't want you to worry about *that,* on top of everything else. As a matter of fact, don't worry at all. If I can't get $50 out of Retch, I'll get $25 or know the reason why. Good night."

XV
Le Décor

It was all, Mr. Blandings decided several days later, a blessing in disguise, at least in a sort of way. It had cost a lot of money, but in exchange for it he had newly acquired a pliant spouse, quiet, co-operative, deferential. And perhaps it would not cost so much money after all. Mr. Simms, internally relieved by the lecture he had given his clients, had telephoned to say that he had read the riot act to Mr. Retch for putting so literal a construction on the whims and vagaries of an owner's wife; that furthermore Mr. Retch was yearning, as Paolo had once yearned for Francesca, to get the contract for the $85,000 mansion that a wealthy garter-belt manufacturer was soon to build no more than fifteen miles from Bald Mountain—and that if Mr. Blandings were to write this gentleman a letter whose well-thought-out spontaneities expressed an admiration for Mr. Retch's unwavering rectitude as a contractor, it might well be discovered that Mr. Retch would be as putty in Mr. Blandings' hands when it came to a discussion of the cost of flower-sink flagstones.

Mr. Blandings did not convey this to his wife; not in full, at least. The opportunity for marital discipline was too bright to tarnish with subjunctives; moreover, Mr. Blandings was enjoying with a deep and satisfying fullness his wife's altered regard for him as man, breadwinner, and intellect. She was to him, once again, as she had been to him when she was a fair young girl; as she had been when she had girlishly courted him with neckties and fudge, or as in the early days of their marriage, when she had sat on his footstool, her arms outflung to embrace his knees, her adoring gaze turned upward to catch his lightest utterance. It had been a long time ago, thought Mr. Blandings; a long time ago, and a lot had happened. He looked at his wife in the corner; her fair blue eyes were behind reading glasses now; her golden hair was darker and sparser; the simple bun in which she used to wear it dispersed into the complex loops and swirls that she brought home, in new weekly varieties, from the parlors of Vincent & Henri, down the street.

"Sweetheart," said Mrs. Blandings, softly. "I'm—"

It was impossible for her voice to achieve, ever again, the shy tentativeness, the captivating hesitancy that it had had seventeen years ago; but this was not bad, Mr. Blandings thought, not bad at all.

"I'm in the most desperate trouble," he heard his wife conclude.

"What's up?" asked Mr. Blandings, as to his elder daughter.

The color scheme for the house was up. Mr. Simms had called Mrs. Blandings to say that the boss painter was getting finished with his various jobs of sizing and priming the plaster, the woodwork, and the window frames and now wanted to talk turkey about the actual, the final colors. Mrs. Blandings had looked forward all her life to decorating a whole house in exactly the way she wanted it, but now that her lifelong opportunity was at hand she was aghast at the range and freedom it offered her.

"Why don't you just paint all the rooms a nice buff and not fuss about it?" said Mr. Blandings.

The first veil of the New Acquiescence fell from Mrs. Blandings.

"I'm afraid that wouldn't be practicable," she said.

What did seem to her practicable, Mr. Blandings could not discern. His wife had spent a frantic week collecting, rejecting, and recombining color samples from every paint company east of Denver, and studying, with a good many rather offhand dismissals, the choice of colors with which Williamsburg, Virginia, had been restored. She seemed to want something like them but "better," she explained.

There had been a time when the Blandings had assumed that newly purchased furnishings would garnish their home in the country from cellar to garret. Not this hideous stuff of chromium tubing, gold-tinted mirrors, and other breaches of taste, sense, and comfort made in the worship of the word "functionalism"; nothing along the once-promising path that had led its explorers to that inevitable conclusion, the illuminated plastic jukebox. Just solid, sensible, tasteful, and timeless furnishings.

Imperceptibly, this hope had faded; first in the absence of any such furnishings as part of what was then being called "The American Dream"; next, because even if they had existed the costs of home building had left the Blandings nothing but a deficit to cover the budget for any furnishings at all. They had never said a word to one another about this; each merely assumed, and knew that the other shared the assumption, that they would just move up to the country the "city furniture" with which they had been invested at the time of their marriage.

It made Mrs. Blandings a little sad that she could not make a clean sweep of some of their more unfortunate earlier acquisitions, but she bore it bravely; she was now resolved that with brand-new colors, delicate yet bright, masculine yet soft, feminine yet firm, light yet dark, she would accomplish what she had in her mind's eye after all. It was only the interior of the house that bothered her; the exterior was to be an "off-white" with the tiniest imaginable addition of raw umber to give it an almost imperceptible putty tinge. The front door was to be "off-eggplant." The venetian blinds, which had to be painted before they left their own factory, would be further "off" the "off-white" of the house on their outsides; on their insides they would be—gracious, there was so much to think about.

Giving up consultation with Mr. Blandings as no more useful than asking guidance to the True and the Beautiful in a penny arcade, Mrs. Blandings sat down to compose to the boss painter a letter of instructions on which he could not possibly go wrong. That would get him started; then, on the next opportunity for a week end during the relaxing grip of the winter, she could get to her house and have wide swathes of each color painted on the appropriate walls before she gave the final O.K. It was wearing and trying, but that was the way to do it.

"Dear Mr. PeDelford," she began. She bit the pen top and a dreamy look came into her eye as she gathered her powers:

"I am enclosing the samples for the paint colors. To make things so clear that there can be no misunderstanding I will list them below, room by room.

"*Living room.* The color is to be a soft green, not as bluish as a robin's egg, but not as yellow as daffodil buds. The sample enclosed, which is the best I could get, is a little too yellow, but don't let whoever mixes it go to the other extreme and get it too blue. It should just be a sort of grayish apple green.

"*Dining room.* To be yellow, and a very *gay* yellow. Just make it a bright sunshiny color and you cannot go wrong. Ask one of your workmen to get a pound of the A & P's best butter and match it *exactly*.

"*Mr. Blandings' study.* Color must be masculine. The beige sample is quite a bit too pink, so do not follow it literally."

Mrs. Blandings took a new sheet of paper. Whereas her pen had moved haltingly in the beginning it now flew fast; inspiration was upon her.

"*Bedrooms.* These are the only colors that may give you any trouble. For our bedroom I am enclosing a small sample of chintz which I have tagged 'MBR' (Master Bed Room). As you will see, it is flowered, but I do not want you to match any of the flower colors. There are some dots in the background, and it is *these dots* I want the paint to match exactly. The other samples of chintz are for the other bedrooms. The front one, that I call the 'pink room,' is to match the little rosebud next to the delphinium—*not* the one near the hollyhock leaf. The other one, the 'blue room,' should be like the delphinium blossom that is the second from the top on the stem.

"For the guest-room color please match the piece of thread which I have wrapped in the little piece of tissue paper enclosed. *Be careful not to lose it*. I am sorry I cannot send the whole spool, but the store says it is the last spool they have and they cannot get any more, and I have to have it to put the binding on the new slip cover for the green chaise longue. Please be sure to get an exact match, because the whole effect depends on the walls matching the little touches of the same color.

"*Kitchen.* To be white. Not a cold, antiseptic, hospital white, however. It should have a warm effect, but it should not suggest any color except just pure white.

"*Bathrooms.* In the master bath, the color should suggest apple blossoms *just* before they fall. For the guest bath I am enclosing a pressed forget-me-not flower, which should be a good guide for you except that it should be quite a little lighter. The paint must be easy to wash but it must *not* gleam. I wish you would please . . ."

The rooms got painted. It was surprising how well the rooms got painted, considering an unpromising start. Mr. PeDelford, the boss painter, did not know how to take Mrs. Blandings in the beginning, nor did his ambivalence ever completely disappear. He had a sort of forced and reluctant professional admiration for anyone who had the kind of color sensitivity he did not bump into every day, but he also had a masculine contempt for feminine traffickings with pressed flowers, bits of thread, swatches of chintz, and pounds of butter offered as color samples. "We couldn't take time off to go pickin' wildflowers all over the county to get a match for some of these here," said Mr. PeDelford. "How's this for that back room?" He gestured with a cigar toward a bucket of delicate puce. Half an inch of the cigar's dense ash fell into it, but when Mr. PeDelford stirred the mixture vigorously with a split shingle coated with dead leaves, little or no net change resulted. Generous supplies of oats, dandruff, iron filings, sawdust, and earth kept falling into Mr. PeDelford's paint buckets as the job proceeded, but when Mrs. Blandings got used to the procession of these mishaps she seemed to discover that they somehow made very little difference.

"Oh, dear," said Mrs. Blandings. "I can't tell until I see some of it on the wall."

It turned out that she couldn't tell then, either. "I'll have to wait until it dries," she said. When it dried there was something wrong with it, but it was hard to say what. To Mrs. Blandings it was too dark; to Mr. Blandings it was too light. To Mr. PeDelford it was the finest color that had been mixed since the life and times of Botticelli. Under the pressure of his salesmanship, and his increasingly extravagant remarks about Mrs. Blandings' "color sense," it went on the walls. It was followed, one by one, by its companions, most of which, after innumerable fussings, turned

Half an inch of dense cigar ash fell into a bucket of delicate puce, but little or no change resulted.

out to be almost indistinguishable from the paint company's standard samples, as designated by number and made up in thousand-gallon batches at the factory.

It was restful to visit the house now, Mr. and Mrs. Blandings were happy to discover. The weather was growing milder. The swarming workmen were mostly gone, except for the painters, who produced only a gentle swish and slap, swish and slap, as they covered the walls and woodwork and window frames with their mercifully concealing, connecting, and unifying integuments. The place where apparently a horse had kicked a partition and the marks of repair were a vast spreading stain now softly and silently vanished; the rusts, the little splinters, the gouges and nicks, the marks of haste and carelessness and incapacity, all faded slowly away as the colors spread and glowed.

"It's beginning to look simply *lovely,*" said Mrs. Blandings, whose memory of the episode of the flower-sink flagstones had by now totally vanished. "When will you be getting to work on the floors, Mr. PeDelford?"

The oaken floors, which someday must gleam under their scatter rugs, were dull with ground-in plaster dust, mottled with spilled liquids of various colors and viscosities. The house had not yet been swept out, but at least it had been shoveled out, and the footing was less hazardous.

"They ain't in *my* contract," said Mr. PeDelford with simple innocence.

Indeed they were not, Mr. and Mrs. Blandings discovered. They were not in anybody's contract. They had just been forgotten. No matter how careful even the best architect may be, some things are bound to escape him. Mr. PeDelford allowed as how, since he had his crew right on the site, he could do the floors with stain, wax, and polish for $225. This added one third to the whole painting-contract figure, but Mr. Blandings had been through so much by now that another $225, once a sizable sum, was now little more to him than a theoretical concept, anyway.

He was discovering that getting a house finished was a horror of the same intensity, but of wholly different order, as getting it started. The problems of starting a house were vast, few, and insoluble; the problems of getting one finished were small, multitudinous, and insoluble. Deciding which was worse was like deciding whether you preferred death through being crushed by a bulldozer or torn apart in a threshing machine. By the time the painting was finished, the house was indubitably ninety-five per cent done, and ninety-five per cent of Mr. Retch's requisition payments just as indubitably due him. But a house that was ninety-five per cent finished could not be lived in.

In the living room there was merely a bald gash of brick, mortar, and rough studding surrounding the fireplace; the sections for a plump bolection molding had not come. In the bathroom, lath and plaster showed in recesses prepared for medicine cabinets where there were none. The three crates of lighting fixtures that had arrived for the "Blandings Job" in the days when it was no more than a shower of rocks from Mr. Zucca's dynamite were now discovered to lack collars and bushings without which their final installation was not possible. Hardware was affixed to most doors except those which it was desirable to keep closed against the weather. One ganglion of electrical cable awaited its stove, and a chasm in the midst of order marked a kitchen cabinet that had arrived crumpled like an old shoebox. Its substitute would arrive someday, and might then be installed, but the whiteness of its enamel would be a different whiteness from the whiteness of all the others, Mrs. Blandings well knew, and there would never be anything to do about it, except grow old with it as gracefully as possible in the spirit of Browning's Rabbi Ben Ezra. . . .

If there was anything in the world that Mr. and Mrs. Blandings now wanted to see it was their house, its outside painted. Until it was painted they would not know whether they liked it or not, whether the whole vast project was a success or a failure. With bare brick, bare wood, bare copper, bare galvanized iron all showing in their native states and colors, the Blandings could not see their house steady or see it whole.

But Mr. PeDelford could not paint the outside of the house. Four long pieces of redwood siding near the eaves were missing; enough had been split or damaged in handling to make Mr. Retch's supply short by just that much. The mill would supply him when next he had a big enough job to make delivery and handling worth-while. In their absence, the final moldings could not go on; in the meantime Mr. PeDelford's painters betook themselves to other quarters, to return God knew when.

One late afternoon as the sun was fading and the Blandings were contemplating the glories that might someday be their household, the house was seized with a convulsive and sustained shudder. Mrs. Blandings cried out; Mr. Blandings made an elaborate pretense of calm. The seizure lasted a long half minute, and passed away. Before the Blandings left, the same racking spasm again shook their home from ridge to footing. They could feel the coarse tremor in the walls; the plaster dust, still unswept, danced in the floor cracks. Mr. Blandings, reporting by an alarmed telephone call to Mr. Simms, found it so difficult to describe the convulsion that Mr. Simms could only say he would come over and investigate as soon as he could: other homes for other people were beginning to be on his mind and his drawing board, he gently implied; the Blandings must begin to realize that soon the house would be theirs, and the problems of its everyday existence would then become their problems, not his.

When Mr. Simms got around to visiting the house, it stood serene and still; no such visitation as the Blandings had described could even remotely be imagined. After a week of periodic visits, it at last obliged with its seizure late one afternoon, as owners and architect were about to give up their vigil. Mr. Simms then swiftly traced it to the oil burner, starting up in answer to the call of its thermostat as the afternoon warmth faded from the air of an equinoxial day. The bolts that held its motor base to the concrete had never been screwed home; this, plus a flutter in the smoke-pipe damper, had set every inch of hot-air duct to quivering as the motor first revolved. Mr. Simms, with a wrench for the motor bolts and a piece of twisted wire for the pipe damper, banished the ague in five minutes.

"If I were you, I'd start doing things like that for myself," he said. "That's one way; the other way is to spend two hours tracing John Retch on the telephone and then waiting another three to ten days before he gets a man back here to find out what it's all about. Then you have another little extra for adjustment work that Retch can claim was outside the contract. You'll find a lot of loose screws around, here and there; you can either tighten 'em yourself or spend $25 to bring a man thirty miles with a screw driver. I know which I'd do if I were you."

He cleared his throat; he had intended to say nothing more, but perhaps this was the best occasion, he would ever have for a *Nunc Dimittis*.

"If you don't mind my saying so, one of the

hardest jobs an architect has is weaning the owner when the time comes. I hope I'll always be seeing a lot of you, for after all I don't live far away—and I'm very proud of this house, I don't mind confessing. But these other people whose plans I have on my drawing board right now—they stand about where you and your plans stood a year ago. They want to see a good deal of me—do you remember how it was?"

Yes, Mr. Blandings thought, with a sigh, he had a house; now he must grow up to it. It was his, to have and hold forever as the Deed had said—subject, of course, to the advice and consent of the Seagate-Proletarian Savings Bank. His cares were not ending, it appeared, but, in a realer sense, just beginning. He mopped his brow and told Mr. Simms that indeed he understood.

As part of his new responsibilities, Mr. Blandings began to contemplate his house from a new vantage point. It didn't just sit there and exist, he suddenly came to realize, but fumed and hummed like a battleship at anchor. He began a methodical round of all equipment designed to flow, spin, or reciprocate. There was a lot of it.

The turning on of a tap produced spasmodic and occasionally violent gushes of a liquid that was the color of weak coffee but fizzed like champagne. He assumed that this condition would someday right itself, and turned his attention to one of his brand-new, unbelievably filthy toilet bowls yet to know the brush or the determination of Woman. It was the newest and most inaudible type known to science.

Mr. Blandings with slight timidity pushed the flush lever on the stylishly low porcelain tank. The toilet acknowledged a human impulse with an almost imperceptible click, and then the waters in its uncleansed bowl began a silent, lovely swirl; implacable but beyond the limits of human audibility. This is marvelous, Mr. Blandings thought. Hitherto, when he activated a toilet, he had been accustomed to that same melancholy, long, withdrawing roar that Matthew Arnold had first observed and commented upon at Dover Beach in the midst of the disenchantment of Victorian England. The swirling waters gathered themselves up, silently still, and sluiced themselves, by a miracle of quiet abnegation, out of his sight forever. Without warning there then emerged from the toilet's deepest inwardness so harsh and terrifying a yawp as to make Mr. Blandings leap backwards into the hall. He tried all the other toilets, and was similarly rewarded, first by the enigma of the silent whirlpool, then by the horror of the final, climactic withdrawal. From his pocket he pulled a little notebook labeled "House Notes" and in it he wrote a pungent criticism, for Mr. Simms's benefit, of what he had just observed. It was full of a dozen close-packed pages already, but he knew that after a while he would tear them all up, and that in a year or two he would get used to the toilets and to the progress they exemplified, as he would to everything else in life that promised richly, and petered out.

XVI
Possession

The day came at last when the Blandings' house was to become the Blandings' house, and none other's. The ceremony of the architect's final certification and the owner's acceptance was at hand. Eight long weeks had gone by in the Blandings' lives while the percentage of the house's completion moved with glacial speed from an estimated ninety-five per cent to an even more empirically calculated ninety-eight. There, presumably, it would stay forever, except as the Blandings spent another several hundred dollars to do at their own expense what Mr. Retch vowed passionately he would do when he had "a moment"—something apparently never in history destined to arrive. Bill Cole, who still discussed the "possibilities of resale" with Mr. Blandings, had insisted on an endless legal hocus-pocus before giving Mr. Retch his final check. Mr. Blandings was to give it to *him,* not to Mr. Retch. Bill Cole was then to notify Mr. Retch that he had the check, signed and certified and ready for delivery, and would hand the same over to Mr. Retch on the conditions following and to wit, namely. There had here followed such an impenetrable forest of verbiage that even Mr.

Blandings thought his friend Bill Cole was carrying things too far. Then he thought of what the Messrs. Barratry, Lynch & Virgo had done to him in the days while he was waiting, wasted and pale, for his mortgage money, and he relaxed again. It was Mr. Retch's turn to fume. Somehow, Mr. Blandings felt, Mr. Retch fumed to better effect than he; after only a few days of it, and without any notable improvements in the real world of bolts and butts and catches and cabinets, for which the Blandings were still waiting, Bill Cole suddenly said that everything was now all right: the check could be passed. The check was passed.

So now Mr. Blandings and his wife were on their way to possess their house, and it was once again the flowering spring. Mr. Blandings drove through lanes of dogwood and banks of violets and dripping bushes of forsythia, and smiled at the recollection of how, once upon a time, he had lost himself in a tangle of back-country roads when first he had set out to find his sanctuary unaided by the real-estate man. Now his practiced twists and turns took him toward the goal without any intervention of his conscious mind whatever.

The last turn was made. The Blandings saw their house and a cry escaped them. It was a cry of joy. Mr. PeDelford's work was completed; there stood their creation in all its gleaming whiteness, the delicate waving leaves of the Hackett maples the perfect offsetting foils. The house was lovelier than the fairest drawings that ever Mr. Simms had drawn. It seemed to wait for them as a girl would wait, with downcast eyes, for her lover's first shy kiss.

The entrance to the citadel was not accomplished with ease; the house appeared, on closer examination, to be more like a full-rigged ship, floating becalmed on a sea of mud. ". . . and grade to a line ten feet out from foundations of house in all directions," the Blandings' contract had said, as a sort of valedictory. This Mr. Retch had duly done, leaving beyond the ten-foot line a rich miscellany of surpluses from the plumbing, heating, carpentry, and mason trades. Where the grading had been accomplished, the warm spring rains had liquefied the results. But once across this moat, the Blandings removed their ruined shoes and stood with reverence in their stocking feet upon their gleaming oaken floors. . . .

Of course, there were little misfortunes here and there. The fireplace's bolection molding, now that it was finally in place, was nothing like what Mrs. Blandings had had in her mind's eye from the beginning. The suave, silent mercury switches in the lighting system had all been ripped out and replaced with switches whose onward *click* and offward *clack* had the attention-commanding value of a circus clown's slapstick: a three-wire master-switch arrangement on which Mr. Blandings had insisted, whereby he could turn all the hall and stair and outside lights on with one finger at night if he smelled a smell or heard a sound, had made their use impossible, but nobody had told him, or given him a chance to revise his wishes.

The "very advanced" fluorescent lighting in the dining room hummed so loudly from its hidden ballasts in the lighting cove that conversation would obviously not be possible. "We have never recommended this type of fluorescent lighting equipment for rooms of low noise level," the Nadir Electric Supply Company wrote tartly in answer to Mr. Blandings' protest. "Had your contractor informed us of the use contemplated for this equipment we would have warned against it. A system of lead washers and asbestos shields, if properly installed, might obviate your trouble somewhat." It was later discovered that the lighting turned a healthy roast of beef into a purple mass of putrescence on the dining table and the whole installation was eventually removed and replaced by the more conventional type of lamp invented by Thomas Alva Edison in 1879.

A well-meaning heating engineer from the Radiant-Happiness people, makers of the Blandings' oil burner, had contributed his mite. He had visited the premises in the days of construction and, in the sweet name of Service, had ruined the Blandings' hopes for the "rumpus room" they had planned at a later day to create in their cellar: observing that his company's gorgeously enameled creation was placed so that the diverging radii of its arms were not of equal length, he had persuaded Mr. Retch to move it into the middle of the cellar "so these good people will get equal Radiant-Happiness heating in all their rooms." Mr. Retch had looked at Mr. Simms's plans, which indicated no reason why not, and had complied. The heater was now implacably anchored in the concrete. Mr. and Mrs. Blandings had looked at it there a dozen times before: only now did its significance dawn upon them.

One boner by the otherwise flawless Mr. Simms was disconcerting: in changing the location of the electric hot-water heater on the plans one hot night of a summer now long gone by, he had relocated the water lines but forgotten to specify electrical connections to the new position; in all the days that followed neither he nor owners, nor builder, nor plumber, nor electrical contractor, nor any other mortal soul had noticed the oversight—until the Blandings turned on their first hot-water tap. A good deal of cellar wiring had to be ripped out and put in again to permit the new stretch of heavy power cable to run from the busses to the heater, and Mr. Simms had insisted that the $85 involved be deducted from his fee.

There was, too, the window hardware which would not work.

There was, too, the window hardware which would not work, and the one bathroom floor to which the linoleum would not adhere even under the furthest refinements of third-degree pressure. All the doors stuck except those that would not latch at all; several were hung to open the wrong way, and one (in the cellar) would open only a meager distance before its swing was blocked by the air duct which had been altered in the cause of Mrs. Blandings' flower-sink flagstones.

Perhaps it was the paint that disturbed Mrs. Blandings most of all. She had achieved a pretty fair approximation of the colors of apple blossoms about to fall, of forget-me-nots in desiccation, with which she had faced the skeptical Mr. PeDelford, but in her eagerness for soft and delicate colors she had either misunderstood or never heard a mumbled and ambiguous warning from her boss painter. She had a horror of gloss in her colors, so there was none; it had not occurred to her that in the absence of any varnish in the paint mixture, the coats as they dried on the wall would become culture surfaces for thumbprints. She could not touch one of her own delicate and ultra-cleanly finger tips to a wall without producing an effect as if a bootblack had splayed his palm against it.

There was also the insect world to cope with. The spring was still early and the screens were on the windows, but it was nevertheless apparent that Mrs. Blandings' paints held a deep fascination for *Culex pungens*, *Musca domestica*, and assorted *Coccinellidae* and *Phyllophagae*. They had hurled themselves upon it in assault wave after assault wave, and it was theirs.

But the Blandings had built a good house—a very fine house indeed, by any standards that anyone might wish to apply. Someday soon, Mr. Blandings would have time, he vaguely thought,

She could not touch one of her ultra-cleanly hands to a wall without producing an effect as if a bootblack had splayed his palm against it.

to consider its process of morphology more at length than he now felt disposed to do. The ovum from which all had sprung, he vaguely remembered, had been the old Hackett farmhouse on which $10,000 was to be spent for "restoration." The larva was the $15,000 house that Mr. Simms had begun to design. The pupal stage was reached when Mr. Retch began to build something for a contract price of $26,991.17. The eventually emerged dwelling in full adult form bore, as in all other organic processes, little resemblance to its embryo, either to the aesthete's or the cost accountant's eye. Only Mr. Blandings, and he not altogether, would someday know how much money he had really spent on Bald Mountain, compared to the $20,000 concept for land and building with which all had begun. In the far, far back of his head, there rang a figure of $51,000 which he preferred, for the moment, not to examine further.*

* *Mr. Blandings would later discover that the figure his mind bore in upon him might more rightfully have been $56,263.97. Like all figures having to do with homes in the country, this one was arbitrary, since it did not include the days to come of barn repair, driveways, landscaping, boughten and transplanted trees, lawn seed, repairs to fences, the setting out of shrubs and bushes, tree surgery, restoration of orchards, etc. A whole new world of creativity, and the expenses therefor, was not yet, at this stage, open to him. He was also destined to acquire a Cow, before whom the best accountancy minds of Lybrand, Ross Brothers and Montgomery, Ernst & Ernst, Price, Waterhouse & Co., et al., have for years been known to quail.*

XVII
Fulfillment

The Christmas House Number of *The Home Lovely (Combined with House & Home)* lay before Mr. Savington Funkhauser, A.I.A., who was wondering why, after a hard day at the drafting board, he had opened it at all.

"Our problem was to create a home of modern implications in a community dominated by fine old colonial farmhouses that had stood the test of Revolutionary days and before," he read, "and to accent a youthful spirit without adverse repercussions to the traditions of those stout forebears whose indomitable strivings have been the heritage of . . ."

"Spittle," said Mr. Funkhauser in a toneless voice, aloud. He looked for a title at the top of the page to tell him what he was reading. In thin, swash lettering he saw "*Home Lovely*'s December House-of-the-Month Is Tribute to Taste and Ingenuity with Materials Old and New." There seemed here no conveyance of information whatsoever, and Mr. Funkhauser would have tossed the magazine aside save that he could not rouse himself quite enough.

"It was a challenge to our ingenuity," he read on, in a sort of mild hypnosis, "but my husband

and I tackled the difficulties with a will, and out of a combination of carefully budgeted planning, a determination to keep our primary objectives ever before us, and the most friendly three-way cooperation among architect, owner, and builder, we were able to achieve our aims with a minimum of those unforeseen items of expense that occasionally mar the joys of building that *sine qua non* of all normal couples' ideals and ambitions, the Home of One's Own."

"Whose bilge *is* this?" Mr. Funkhauser asked of the fireplace. On the instant, a picture caption answered him: "Mrs. J. Holocoup Blandings, whose delightful mountain dwelling is this month's *Home Lovely* Choice as . . ."

Mr. Funkhauser's right arm moved suddenly, and the Christmas House Number described a graceful arc, disappearing into the tall, chromium-bound cylinder of simulated-walrus Nutasote which served Mr. Funkhauser as a waste receiver. A moment later the young architect fished it out again, and turned back to the Assistant Editor's interview with "the *chic* and attractive Mrs. Blandings, mistress of 'Surrogate Acres.'" For some five wordless minutes he studied the dim half tones and spidery line cuts, arranged ingeniously askew on the chalky paper. Suddenly he came on something familiar, and a flush darkened his face. He muttered for a moment, and then, taking pen and paper, he commenced the draft of a letter:

"Dear Mr. Blandings," he wrote. "In the Christmas issue of *The Home Lovely* I have observed the display of your new residence, and an interview which purports to be with your wife. In it, on page 166, I notice a reference which says '. . . once the impracticalities of an earlier designer had been discarded as wholly unsuitable . . .' I would scarcely have credited this to be a reference to myself, and some work I did for you from which I later withdrew, were it not that on the following page an illustration at the top labeled, 'Discarded Study' is an obvious and offensive caricature of a rendering I submitted to you on—"

Mr. Funkhauser left the date blank for filling in when he went to his filing cabinet to examine the documents bearing on the Funkhauser-Blandings Grievance Case of long ago.

"Taken in conjunction," he resumed, "the sentence and drawing offer to my professional standing an affront and damage which I cannot afford to pass unnoticed. I am in consequence instructing my attorneys, the Messrs. Barratry, Lynch & Virgo, to communicate with you regarding possible steps toward redress which . . ."

Miles away, on Bald Mountain, in the midst of Surrogate Acres, beneath an uninsulated roof

He was dreaming that his house was on fire.

which creaked slightly now and then under the growing snow load of a winter storm, Mr. Blandings smiled uneasily in his sleep. He was dreaming that his house was on fire.

About the Author

ERIC HODGINS made his magazine debut in 1926 with the *Atlantic Monthly*. He served as editor-in-chief of *The Youth's Companion* and associate editor of *Redbook* before being hired by *Fortune*, where his very first job was the exposé of European munitions makers—"Arms and the Men"—of which *The New Yorker* quietly said: "We hereby award it the Pulitzer Prize." In 1937 Hodgins became *Fortune*'s publisher, and by 1938 he had risen in Time Inc., to the position of vice-president. In April 1946, he resigned his post to go back to the writing career he had mislaid during the thirties.

Mr. Blandings Builds His Dream House, first fruit of Hodgins' return to writing, was born as a short story in *Fortune* early in 1946. He had previously written three books of scientific popularization, but *Mr. Blandings* is totally unlike anything he had done before. Or, you might say, unlike anything anyone has ever done before.

Center Point Publishing
600 Brooks Road • PO Box 1
Thorndike ME 04986-0001 USA

(207) 568-3717

US & Canada:
1 800 929-9108
www.centerpointlargeprint.com